I0369496

A VINEYARD BLESSING

THE VINEYARD SUNSET SERIES

KATIE WINTERS

ALL RIGHTS RESERVED. No part of this publication may be reproduced, distributed, or transmitted in any form or by any means, including photocopying, recording, or other electronic or mechanical methods, without the prior written permission of the publisher.

Copyright © 2021 by Katie Winters

This is a work of fiction. Any resemblance of characters to actual persons, living or dead is purely coincidental. Katie Winters holds exclusive rights to this work. Unauthorized duplication is prohibited.

PROLOGUE
30 YEARS EARLIER

AT FIVE YEARS OLD, Beth Leopold knew one thing without a shadow of a doubt: that one day she would don a multiple layered, frilly white dress, carry a ten-pound bouquet of daffodils, pledge her life to a prince, and ride off into the sunset on the back of his sterling white horse. This seemed to be what all of her idols, like Ariel and Belle and Cinderella, had done before her, and Beth saw no reason her life couldn't carry such magic. Happily ever after seemed standard and Beth was ready for it.

Now, as a heavy rain lapped across the glowing windows of her upstairs bedroom, Beth prepared yet another dress rehearsal for such an affair. Teddy bears lined either side of a makeshift "church" aisle; Barbies, dressed in their finest glittering gowns, were tilted against books to be kept upright; her plastic horse collection waited out front, where, one by one, they'd dropped off each of the guests for the royal wedding. "It's the wedding of the century," Beth told them now in a booming voice, one meant to be her father, the king's. "And the entire kingdom has come to see it."

For this ceremony, Beth had selected her most pristine Ken doll, the one with bright blue eyes and wild, beach blonde waves. She'd dressed him in a strapping tuxedo and tilted him against a large pile of her father's books, where he grinned purposefully, his chin tilted upright to see her face. Naturally, Beth had already changed into her wedding best: a purple lace getup her mother had purchased for her from a little boutique in downtown Oak Bluffs. At the time, her mother had called it her "fairy dress" and had even allowed Beth to wear it outside of the store. Once upon the sidewalk, she'd twirled and twirled in place until her skirt billowed up around her.

Outside, Beth's older brother, Kurt, banged against her bedroom door. Beth grew frigid with a strange mix of annoyance and intrigue. She normally took any opportunity to hang with her older brother, as she was fascinated with him and his strange interests and his alarmingly loud video games. Unfortunately, now was a pretty wretched time, as she was smack-dab in the middle of her wedding day. A girl just didn't walk out on her wedding day.

After Kurt howled her name again, Beth scampered over to the door and cracked it open; she couldn't allow Kurt to see what she'd created, as it would dilute the magic.

"Hey. You want to play outside?" Kurt asked it flippantly, as though he'd hoped for another option but had ultimately landed on this.

Beth shifted her weight as Kurt's six-year-old face grew distorted.

"Wait. Why is there so much glitter on your face?"

Beth shivered, suddenly annoyed. "What? There isn't." She

knew very well that there was; she had raided her mother's makeup bag for this very reason.

"Yes, there is." Kurt placed a hand over her door, suddenly sensing she'd hidden something behind it, something she didn't want him to see.

"Don't..."

"You want me to call for Mom?"

Beth didn't want to involve their mother, whose moods seemed to shift as swiftly as the tides. Some days, she was in the mood to purchase Beth a splendorous dress; other days, she blared to her children that she'd never wanted them in the first place, that she should never have been a mother.

With Beth distracted, Kurt blasted the door open to allow him a full view of the wedding ceremony, complete with future-husband, Prince Ken. Beth's stomach twisted as she stewed in resentment for her brother, who couldn't leave well enough alone.

But instead of belittling her, instead of telling her what a fool she was, Kurt stepped into the bedroom, slipped the door closed behind him, and demanded, "I didn't know it was your wedding day. Why didn't you invite me?"

Immediately, Beth felt it. The curtain had lifted on the stage of their imaginative playtime; suddenly, she really was a princess—and Kurt was maybe a knight in the kingdom. Kurt saluted her as Beth fell into a curtsey, which she had practiced several times already that afternoon in preparation for her marriage to the prince.

"It is my honor to be here at the royal ceremony," Kurt told her.

Beth blinked ten times to push the tears back. Reality had folded away from them. Everything seemed to glitter with beauty and love and hope for something brighter than the dark Martha's

Vineyard clouds outside and the even darker moods of their mother, who sat smoking down the hall.

"Shall I walk you down the aisle, Princess Beth?" Kurt asked somberly.

"It would be my pleasure," Beth whispered, her little voice so light and bright. "Thank you for joining me on the happiest day of my life."

CHAPTER ONE

THE LITTLE SAILOR'S Delight Beach Bar on the corner edge of Oak Bluffs hosted karaoke nights every Thursday throughout the autumn, winter, and spring seasons. It worked out to be a bright light in the darkness for those islanders who remained on Martha's Vineyard all year long and didn't, like so many others, depart at the first shift in temperature.

This little bar was the first thing Beth witnessed this particular Thursday in late October when Lola Sheridan drew her hands up from Beth's eyes and screamed, "Surprise!" as the rest of the women who'd kidnapped her at the end of her workday howled with excitement. Beth shivered as the autumn rain flicked its way across her cheek. Was she meant to be excited about karaoke? She'd never sang karaoke in her life.

"Oh, come on," Lola, who was always a warm light of frenetic energy, offered as she swung her arm over Beth's shoulder. "It's not so bad. And Christine will perform for us first, won't you, Christine?"

Christine hobbled forward, her hand-stretched over her pregnant belly. "If you want me to sing all about being the fattest woman on this island, then I'll do it."

"Darling, you're nothing compared to me when I had the twins." This was Claire, who'd birthed Gail and Abby a little over sixteen years ago. "They wouldn't let me onto bridges for fear I would collapse them."

"Actually, that's true. Claire was the reason behind the big Nantucket earthquake of 2005," Charlotte interjected playfully. "I had to hide her from the government after that. They wanted to conduct studies on her."

"Are we going to hover out here forever? Or should we go grab our table?" Susan Sheridan was hidden beneath a massive hood as rain flattened itself over the protective material of her raincoat.

"Let's get you inside." Lola roped her arm through Beth's elbow and hustled her up the front steps and into the quaint establishment, where a waitress directed them to a large table, set up toward the side of the restaurant, with good access to the makeshift karaoke stage up front.

As Beth slipped out of her coat, Kelli ran in from the rain, leafed through her bag, and then drew out a large, bright white hat with a silly veil attached. On the hat read the words: **BRIDE TO BE**. She placed it delicately upon Beth's raven hair and then clapped her hands joyously.

"Have you ever seen a more beautiful bride?" Kelli cried.

Beth blushed as fear crept across her stomach. When she'd left her work at the hospital that evening, she'd anticipated a restful evening at home with her nine-year-old son, Will, complete with delivery pizza and whatever movie he wanted to watch the most. She suppressed a yawn as she tried to discover her voice.

"This is really all too much," she told everyone.

"Honey, no way. We do things big in the Montgomery family," Charlotte stated as she collected herself in the chair across the table. "I know you keep telling me that you want to keep your wedding small..."

"Just family and friends," Beth interjected, her tone shifting.

"But you know I'm a wedding planner," Charlotte continued, as though she hadn't said anything. "And I can bring whatever magic you've dreamed of. Come on. Didn't you dream of your wedding day when you were a little girl? Didn't you think about your dress and the ceremony and all the people there to just see you on the happiest day of your life?"

"You're good," Amanda Sheridan said coyly as she removed her coat and snuck in alongside Charlotte. "You've got your sales pitch all worked out."

"Oh, come on now." Charlotte grimaced, playfully slapping her hand.

"Yeah, yeah. I know. My wedding was a disaster," Amanda remarked with a half-smile as a strange wave of what seemed to be resentment and fear passed over her face. It fell away quickly as she righted herself, grabbed the menu from the center of the table, and muttered, "I hope they have gin and tonic. I'm craving a gin and tonic."

"Seriously, Beth. Whatever you want, we can make it happen," Charlotte offered, her eyes widening. "My baby brother Andy—

well, you know that we never thought we'd ever get him back. The fact that he's here... and he's marrying an island girl..."

"It's just about more than we can stand," Claire cried.

Beth's heart drummed in her throat. How could she explain it to them? That so long ago, she'd dreamed of fairytales; she'd believed in magic. That was before the war had taken her brother, Kurt, from the world. It was a time before she'd had a whirlwind summer affair that had left her a single mother, before Will's autism diagnosis. It was before her life operated in continuous before and after's.

Her love for Andy was impossibly beautiful. It was far more than she'd ever envisioned for herself. It seemed like too much to ask the universe that she was allowed to marry him at all, and besides, over the previous ten years, she'd essentially kept to herself. Save for a friend here and there, she didn't have many to invite to any kind of wedding. The Sheridan and Montgomery families were just about it in terms of wedding guests.

Their waitress was playful and funny, trying to pick at Beth like the other girls, asking her about her engagement and the day of her approaching wedding.

"Between Thanksgiving and Christmas! As though there isn't enough going on...." the waitress joked.

Beth's cheeks burned. It had been Andy's idea to slip the wedding in between everything else. Andy had had a whole lot of ideas lately. His idea to finally move in together was a frequent topic, one that caused her stomach to stir with fear of disappointment and anxiety of the unknown. All the while, Andy remained at that shoddy apartment, awaiting her "call." What was she waiting for? And what would happen when she said, "I do"?

Wives and husbands were meant to live together, to make decisions together. But in the previous month or so, Beth had felt herself grow uncertain, nervous and riddled with fear.

Lola ordered them a long list of appetizers, declaring that she was "utterly starving." Amanda piped in to suggest that they also order onion rings, as she had a craving for them. Lola's eyes jumped up toward Amanda's as she muttered, "Craving? Are you kidding me? Don't tell me you went the way of Audrey..."

Amanda's eyes bugged out. "Aunt Lola! No way. I've spent all week eating salads and just want a little grease, is all."

"How are things going with Sam, anyway?" Claire asked, leaning forward onto the table to burrow into the gossip circle.

Amanda's cheeks burned bright red as the waitress beckoned for them to order all their drinks so she could get the orders to the bartender.

"Come on, girls! I know you're hankering to sing. And there's nothing like liquid courage to get it going," the waitress said.

Beth ordered herself a white wine while the others focused on cocktails and fruity drinks. It was a bachelorette party, for goodness sake— Beth's, in fact, and everyone wanted to sizzle with the adrenaline of another person's life-changing decision. Beth hardly touched her wine; sometimes, if she drank too much, she grew jittery and nervous, even more than she already was.

"But what will you wear?" Claire demanded joyously. Nobody seemed to guess the darkness that swirled within Beth's stomach.

Beth hummed and hawed. "I have a few ideas." This was a lie.

"Come on. You have to let us take you shopping," Charlotte interjected.

Beth wanted to tell them that actually, money wasn't entirely a

"I don't know what to do with them," Lola remarked with a funny glance back toward Beth.

Could Beth be light and free the way the Sheridan and Montgomery girls seemed to be? She knew they'd gone through their own share of hardships; still, they had one another and lifted each other out of the darkness. She'd never had anyone else to do that. In the wake of Kurt's death, even her parents had turned away from her, growing increasingly obstinate and dark. She'd felt she had no one, that is, until Will was born.

He'd been her purpose. He'd been her life.

"Come on, Beth. Get up here!" This was Lola, back on the microphone and eager to get Beth involved in the festivities. "What do you think? Britney Spears? Fugees? ABBA?"

"Oh! ABBA! Let's all do ABBA!" This was Claire, who popped up from the other side of the breadsticks and hustled to the stage, beckoning for the rest of them to come up.

Kelli tapped Beth's shoulder and said, "They'll pester you to do this until you do, you know. You might as well do it with everyone else."

Beth tried to hide behind the more expressive Lola and Christine, who placed their hands on their hearts as they belted out, "Mamma Mia." Beth mouthed along with the words without putting forth any actual noise. Nobody sensed anything was off. In the crowd, people clapped around, their eyes glittering with excitement. Apparently, the Montgomery-Sheridan clan put on a pretty good show.

Back at the table, Lola suggested they grab another round of drinks before saying that really, they should form a family band. Beth took a sip of her water and glanced at her phone to get a sense of the time. When they'd initially kidnapped her from work, Christine had whispered not to worry, that they'd hired Denise, her typical babysitter, to make sure Will was all right.

When Beth flashed on her phone, however, she saw that Denise had called her ten times and texted her twelve.

DENISE (BABYSITTER): Hey! Call me.

DENISE (BABYSITTER): It's just that Will won't calm down.

DENISE (BABYSITTER): It seems different than the other times.

DENISE (BABYSITTER): I'm really sorry to bother you at your bachelorette party. But I really need your help.

CHAPTER TWO

"INHALE. Exhale. Feel the oxygen as it flows throughout your body. Let go of anything that's holding you back from being your truest self."

Andy furrowed his brow, dropped his head back, then immediately erupted from the end of his bed and stabbed a finger against his phone, ending the meditation course he'd downloaded for the morning. His therapist had suggested mediation as a way to dig into his body, make peace with some of the strange weather in his head, and dive into the new day with a fresh perspective. Thus far, he'd just felt the words to be hokey; the experience felt belittling. If meditation was supposedly a "healthy thing," maybe he would stick to fried chicken and beer. It made him happy, at least.

Andy pressed the power button on his coffee maker and hovered in the dark shadows of his kitchen. It was a week before Halloween, and on the counter, he'd positioned a small bowl of Reese's candies, all wrapped up in their golden sleeping bags, awaiting their sweet release. After he poured his first mug of coffee, he contemplated digging his teeth into an early-morning chocolate. He glanced at his physique as he remained in a pair of boxers and nothing else and soon thought better of it. He was still rather toned from his years in the army, and he wanted to retain that over the next six weeks, prior to his wedding to the love of his life.

Beth. Beth Leopold. He'd loved her since he'd met her all those years ago when she'd been just the unattainable sister of Kurt Leopold, his dearest best friend and a man the war had taken from him all the way back in 2005.

Andy had met Beth for the second time the previous December in the wake of his father's car accident. At that time, his family had called him back from his wayward life in Boston, where he'd felt he would just live out the rest of his days alone. He had arrived to a tumultuous Martha's Vineyard, learned that his departure had created a rift in many of his family members, and ultimately helped to get Kelli out of the marriage he'd always secretly thought was violent, either emotionally or physically. Throughout that time, he'd learned the depths of Beth's own sorrows— the fact that her family had all passed on and that she'd lived as a single mother for the previous eight years, alone with the weight of the world on her shoulders.

They had needed each other.

As the box was low, Andy poured himself half a bowl of cereal, a little bit of milk, and leaned over the counter to munch on his breakfast. The apartment in which he now lived wasn't much to write home about— just what he could afford in the wake of his departure from his parents' place. He and his father had mended their relationship to a point, but Andy had sensed if he remained within Trevor Montgomery's walls, their heads would find new ways to butt all over again. When he'd taken the six-month lease on this very apartment, he had assumed he would only be there three or four months, tops. Things with Beth had been so fluid, so easy that they'd already discussed moving in together in February.

Why, then, had Beth's resistance to the idea grown thicker?

Andy had only recently grown accustomed to the idea that his phone was something he had to check on frequently. In recent years, he'd been a pariah from society, not exactly the type of guy who had any correspondence to check up with. Now, his phone buzzed all over again, a reminder that he was a part of another world, and that world demanded something from him, even this early in the morning.

The text messages were all from his sisters. They began last night around eleven and continued till the early morning. Now, Kelli had texted him again, causing his phone to ding.

CLAIRE: Andy? Pick up your phone! There's something up with Beth.

CHARLOTTE: Andy, we're out with Beth for her bachelorette. Something's wrong with Will. She had to run home. Can you go over there and check on her? She's not letting us help at all.

KELLI: Hey, bro. Beth's very upset. I wanted to let you know that she might need you ASAP.

Andy's blood pressure skyrocketed. Immediately, he dialed Beth's phone and waited with bated breath as the rings blared out between his apartment and her tiny home. After five rings, the phone went straight to voicemail. Fear immediately took over as he thought the worst. He leaped toward his bedroom, donned a pair of jeans, a sweater, and his autumn hat. Meanwhile, he dialed Beth, again and again, praying she would answer soon. Maybe she'd had to take Will to the hospital? Why hadn't she personally texted him to let him know what was going on?

In the car, Andy's thoughts ran rapid with the most outrageous thoughts. Stoplights and stop signs seemed superfluous; he hovered for the briefest second at a four-way intersection before blaring through it, half-praying no sleepy Vineyard police officer hid around the corner.

Will was just about the sweetest little kid anyone could get to know. He was a nine-year-old with a propensity for dinosaur facts and reading and drawing little pictures for Andy, which Andy had hanging now on his fridge. Will's autism was beside the fact. He was simply a remarkable human, one Andy felt proud to know and to (very soon) help raise.

Throughout the summer, as he and Beth had grown closer and Andy had drummed up the courage to ask her to be his wife, Andy had found himself assisting here and there with parent-like Will-related decisions— things like picking Will up from club meetings and helping him with his projects. They'd built a bird feeder together and made their own guacamole, and researched how to craft the perfect paper airplane, which had ultimately failed. When Will grew finicky or exasperated, Andy tried to assist as well, but each time, Beth had swooped in, manning her role perfectly and making Andy feel just like a playmate rather than her partner. Andy had yearned to question her about this— to ask when and how he could begin to play at least part-time dad. Naturally, it was difficult for her to gauge. It had only been her and Will against the world. Andy didn't want to step on her toes.

But if Will had had some kind of emergency last night, she should have reached out. He loved them both, dammit.

His tires screeched to a halt outside of Beth's little house. All the lights were on, overly bright against the grey softness of the morning. Her car remained in the driveway, which lent Andy at least the smallest portion of relief. Will wasn't in the hospital. Perhaps his sisters had blown everything out of proportion.

Andy knocked twice on the front door before Beth pulled it open the slightest bit. Her eyes were lined red, her cheeks hung low, and she smelled slightly sour, as though she'd spent the previous hours sweating and panicked. Embarrassment sizzled across her face. She didn't look pleased to see him. In the background, a slow growl hummed; it sounded like a wild animal.

"Hi, Andy," Beth spoke as though he was a stranger.

"Beth..." He wanted to throw his arms around her. He wanted her head pressed tenderly against his chest. But there was a distance between them.

Before he could speak, there was a clatter from the kitchen. Beth leaped back and hustled down the hall. The door swung open a bit more, with Andy still hovering outside.

"Will! Put that down!" Beth's voice was high-pitched and exhausted.

Andy filled his lungs and pressed his fingers against the door to open it wider. Beth needed him. He could sense the urgency in her face and the strain of her body. Perhaps she was too embarrassed to ask for it? Perhaps she hadn't considered the fact that he could help?

"Will!"

Another crash rang from wall to wall, and then Will let out a half-crazed wail. Andy could hear Beth crying along with him. He closed the door and hustled to the kitchen area, where he found Will in a crumpled heap on the floor with Beth over the top of him, trying her best to hold onto him as it seemed, the world crashed around them. Plates were shattered in every direction; a broom was tipped against the wall, as though Beth had attempted, for a while, to keep up with the manic whirlwind.

"It's okay, baby. It's okay," Beth cooed gently. Her words were so dramatically different than the view around them. It was clear that nothing was okay.

Will cried out again. He sounded like a child version of a pterodactyl, one of the dinosaurs Will had spoken about endlessly over the summer. Andy had seen Will have mini-panics. They were customary in the life of an autistic child. This was something else. This was a hurricane.

"Beth? Can I get you something?" Andy felt so helpless. How could he ever be her husband or Will's father when all he could do was stand there with his arms hanging at his sides?

Will cried out again in alarm. He twisted his head up so that his eyes caught Andy's. "What's he doing here?" he demanded, needling Andy in a way he'd never done.

"Shhh. It's okay, baby. He's leaving soon."

Andy's heart dropped into his stomach. Resistant to the idea, knowing full well he could lose it if he stepped out of the door, he reached for the broom and began to sweep up the shattered pieces of plate, all of which glittered menacingly.

But as he scraped the shards of glass into the dustbin, Beth yanked her head up, made eye contact with him, and muttered, "Andy. Did you not hear me?"

Andy's heart dropped into his stomach. "Just let me clean this up for you before I go."

On cue, Will hurled out another wild cry. Beth's eyes grew wider. "Andy. Please. Go."

Terrified, Andy stepped back toward the doorway. His shoe found a shard of the plate, and it blasted into smithereens beneath him. The sound frightened Will yet again, and he writhed beneath Beth like an animal.

"Please, Andrew. Please," Beth pleaded.

Andy closed his eyes as the pain of this moment overtook him. He felt terribly small. "Just call me when you can and let me know if you need anything— anything at all."

Beth didn't answer him. Andy's stomach felt hollowed out. He walked down the hallway and back into the chill of the morning, at a complete loss. When the door clicked closed behind him, he turned back and with this turn, encountered a whole host of beautiful memories. There on that stoop, he'd kissed Beth Leopold goodnight countless times; he'd given Will the kinds of hugs he'd thought were reminiscent of father-son relationships; he'd thought to himself, "This could be my home one day." Now, the house seemed merely an outline of something he couldn't have. It was a territory in which he didn't belong.

It was six weeks from the wedding, and suddenly, Andy felt like a stranger in the relationship. He had spent the previous sixteen years feeling like something of a stranger within his old life prior to his return to the Vineyard. For this reason, the emotion of it felt like an old friend. Why had he ever assumed everything would be all right? Why had he assumed he could have any version of happily ever after?

CHAPTER THREE

AN INVISIBLE MAGNETISM pulled Andy westward and south toward the old Aquinnah Cliffside Overlook Hotel. Kelli and Xavier's crew were hard at work on the restructuring of the old hotel, working tirelessly before winter's brutality pushed them to stop. Throughout his teenage years, Andy had always been drawn to his eldest sister. He'd sought refuge at her house when he and his parents had squabbled; he'd felt a safety in her gaze unmatched anywhere else.

He parked his car at the far edge of the little makeshift lot, where he could witness the brevity of the task-at-hand. The old hotel was little more than a trashed-out haunted house these days. Its former glory had been lost in the hurricane of 1943. At the time, his grandfather, Robert Sheridan, had been the stand-in hotel manager and his grandmother, Marilyn, had been a guest. Their secrets had just spilled to the surface recently. Marilyn had been married to a man named James, who'd purchased the hotel just before its collapse. In the span of a few days, James had lost his glorious old-world hotel and his beautiful wife. The terror of it had sent him back to New York City, where he'd lived a happy life, escaping from the shadows of this island. Marilyn and Robert had gone on to own the Sunrise Cove Inn before their untimely deaths, which had resulted in Wes Sheridan and Anna Sheridan taking over. Strange that the seed from which everything had sprung lurked here, within the walls of this dilapidated hotel on the edge of the cliffs.

Kelli stood over a large table, muttering to herself as she analyzed the old blueprints for the previous version of the hotel. Her new boyfriend and the owner of the property, Xavier Van Tress, stood alongside her, gesturing to a space of the blueprint with a powerful hand. Andy hadn't spent much time with Xavier and had initially cast him out as an overly rich bigot, the sort of man who whipped his money around as a form of personality and to gloat about. Naturally, Andy was protective over Kelli, especially after everything that had happened with her ex-husband, Mike. Women were drawn to particular types of men. He could only pray she hadn't discovered another bully, one apt to tug her under.

"Andy!" Kelli lifted her eyes to find him as he made his way across the stones of the property. In the distance, a whack-whack-whack resounded as workers tore out several unsteady walls within the hotel.

Andy didn't have the strength to respond. Kelli lifted her chin to whisper something into Xavier's ear before she turned away from the table and made a beeline for Andy. She pressed a hand against his upper arm as her eyes dug into his. If there was anything his eldest sister could do, it was read him like a book.

"Andy, what's wrong?" She demanded it as though he was on trial.

Andy turned his eyes toward the ground. A sharp-edged wind cut against his cheek. Out there on the cliffs, they were utterly exposed.

"You saw Beth?"

"Yes."

The crinkle between Kelli's eyebrows deepened. "She looked so panicked last night. She ran out of the bar before any of us knew what was up. We had all been drinking and nobody noticed she wasn't. It was as though she just couldn't loosen up, or maybe she didn't want to." Kelli shrugged. "Maybe she has a lot going on, or we just overwhelmed her. You know how all us Sheridan-Montgomery women can be at times."

Andy was no longer sure why he'd come. He wanted Kelli to assure him, to tell him everything would shift back into place. But what the heck did Kelli know? Her own life had recently exploded. Time seemed to take advantage of all of them. They had no say.

"Do you want a cup of coffee?" Kelli finally asked when it was clear Andy hadn't the strength to speak.

Kelli led him over to a little breakfast stand they'd set up for the construction workers. There sat a large box of Frosted Delights donuts alongside a large metal container filled with piping-hot coffee. The cardboard top of the box fluttered in the wind. Kelli filled them both styrofoam cups of coffee and gestured toward the donuts. "Help yourself."

Andy couldn't imagine hunger. He coated his tongue with the black liquid, scalding himself.

"I'm worried Beth's having second thoughts."

Kelli shook her head delicately. "Oh, come on. That's impossible."

Andy tried his hand at explaining. "When I showed up at her house this morning, she looked at me like I would never belong in that world. That I could never begin to understand what she and Will have gone through. In a way, it's true. But I've tried my best to learn."

"I saw you were reading a fair number of books about autism this summer at the beach," Kelli remarked as she watched his face from the side.

"And Beth knows I read them..." Andy closed his eyes and sent another blast of liquid death down his throat. "But reading is one thing. Doing is another. And she has to be open to the idea. Heck, I was meant to have moved in by now, but she's always too tired to talk about it. Work gets her down. Then there's Will's mood swings that exhaust her. And it's not like I don't understand. I do. I really do."

"And you have your own host of problems," Kelli pointed out. "If you don't feel like she's supporting you..."

"That's ridiculous," Andy returned.

Kelli's eyes were difficult to read. Andy feared she'd just suggested that Beth wasn't enough for him, either. Was it possible that he had leaped into this too quickly? Perhaps they were both too battered and bruised. Perhaps they were two pieces of two different puzzles, trying to shove themselves together.

"Look, you know I love Beth. I know you love Beth. Maybe today's just a big blip in what will be a beautiful story." Kelli tried to settle his nerves.

Near the blueprint table, Xavier hollered Kelli's name. She excused herself for a moment, rushed back, and spoke with Xavier. He directed her attention to another portion of the blueprints. Andy had the strangest realization that nearly everyone in his life had something to throw their minds into, allowing them to escape from the "real world." Kelli had this new project and her new man. Beth had Will and her career. Andy had lost his seasonal job a few weeks back, with only a half-promise it would be there for him in the spring. With his limited savings, he wasn't entirely sure how he would make ends meet.

Andy felt yet again like a boat without a captain, directionless and hovering above wayward waters.

Kelli reappeared before him, almost without his realizing it, as though he had suddenly blacked out. She tried out a delicate smile and then said, "Want to run a few errands with me? I'd love the company."

A few minutes later, Andy found himself in the passenger seat of Kelli's car. They drove down the makeshift drive that led out toward the main road. Their tires creaked across the stones ominously. Kelli gestured toward the radio and said, "Change it to whatever you want." Andy flicked around for a moment but soon found that nothing suited his aching heart. He again checked his phone for some sign of Beth, but there was nothing.

Kelli dropped off some letters at the post office, then parked at the bank, entered, then exited, all while Andy remained a sad sack in her front seat. The previous months, Andy hadn't felt his old war injury as much; now, the ache of it seemed like an ever-growing scream in the back of his skull.

Kelli's final mission of this morning's round of errands led them

"Andy? You ready?" Kelli called, snapping him out of his reverie.

Andrew turned back to find Clint ogling Kelli with disdain.

"Nothing suit you?"

Kelli grimaced. "A bit out of my price range, for now, I'm afraid."

Clint let out a raucous laugh. "You know the amount of work some of these pieces require?"

Kelli's face grew stony. "I could always come back. I'm just looking..."

"Naw, you don't need to come back," he returned. He then pointed toward the door and coughed. "Here. I'll show you the door. Plenty of half-assed antiques out there in the world for you to put in your little hotel. Have a lovely day."

Andrew recognized this spitting volatility. He suppressed a smile as he followed Kelli out into the grey light of the early afternoon. Once there, Kelli turned the engine on and muttered to herself about the nerve of "some people." Andy had felt a life force within that man, one that he'd seemingly brewed within his own belly. He didn't need anyone in the wide world— only himself and his projects.

CHAPTER FOUR

WILL'S little head dipped deep onto the pillow. His eyes stirred behind his eyelids as he searched for something in his dream. His pajamas were train-themed, with little engines buzzing across the sleeves and the pants, and his hands clenched the exterior of the comforter with a strength that sent shivers down Beth's spine. She'd finally gotten him to sleep after multiple tantrums and countless rounds of tears, the likes of which she hadn't witnessed from her only child in years.

"Poor baby," she hummed now as she swept a hand over his forehead. "Poor, poor baby."

It had been two days, now, since her bachelorette party. Beth had spent much of that time in a delirious state. She hardly remembered Andy stopping by the previous morning. She'd seen him through bleary eyes— a symbol of the tumultuous nature of Will's life and cast him out into the chilly winds of late October. Something in the back of her mind had urged her to tell him to stay.

You need him. Tell him that. But much more of her had heard only the wild cries of her beautiful child and she had dismissed her inner desires for the betterment of her child.

Will had always loved Andy. But in recent weeks, when he had witnessed conversation surrounding Beth's upcoming marriage to Andy, he'd squirmed with panic and frequently fallen into mini-tantrums. Beth had wanted to attribute the horrors to his schooling, to other classmates, to the change in weather. Was she selfish in wanting to marry Andy? Was she selfish in altering Will's life so greatly?

But there was another issue at hand, something she had yearned to dismiss over the previous weeks. It whispered its horrible cries in the back of her mind, an ever-present reminder that life as she'd once known it could very well be over.

Beth paused in the doorway of Will's room to take a final peek at her now-slumbering child. How peaceful he was all tucked in, with his bright stick-on lights glowing across his ceiling. They had stuck them on together years before when Will hadn't been too big for Beth to lift him.

Back in the kitchen, Beth swept up the remaining debris from the plates. She had swept the previous day but wanted to make sure she didn't miss any pieces that Will had shattered. He had used more force than she'd thought he'd had in his little arms, crafting a tidal wave of panic within their small home. After a broom-sweep, she got out the vacuum but soon thought better of it, as she didn't want to wake Will and ignite another attack.

Beth's phone was filled with messages from Andy and Andy's sisters and cousins. It was the Sheridan-Montgomery way to check up on you when things were dark. Just now, Beth's instinct was to find it stifling.

ANDY: Just call me when you can. Don't be afraid to reach out. I love you, Beth. I'm there for you whenever you need me.

Beth dropped onto the ground and curled herself into a ball. She allowed exactly four tears to fall before she righted herself, drank a glass of water, and forced herself to dig through her purse. The afternoon before the bachelorette party, she had driven on her lunch break to the drugstore, where she'd purchased a pregnancy test at the self-check-out station, just to avoid the penetrating eyes of the staff members. Since then, and throughout Will's panic, this pregnancy test had waited for her, burning a hole through the fabric of her purse.

Gosh, hadn't she been careful? Every morning at eight, an alarm blared, and she placed a birth control pill on her tongue and swallowed. It had been every morning, hadn't it? Then again, she and Andy had spent several mornings hiding out in bed together while Will slept on. She had allowed herself to indulge in romance, a thing that had felt like something other people were allowed, not her. Perhaps here and there, she'd taken the pill a little bit late— sometimes a full twelve hours. The pharmacist had said, "Every day, at the same time." Beth was normally so good with directions. Love had made her blind at times.

Beth walked to the bathroom feeling in a kind of nightmare. What the heck would Will feel if she actually was pregnant? He'd already begun to resist the space Andy had taken up in their lives. A new baby would tear through her time and her space. Where would Will fit into any of that? Would the tantrums get worse?

CHAPTER FIVE

ANDY RAPPED his knuckles against the bar counter at the local bar, an act of greeting for the other barflies, who simply nodded. There was a strange, cozy anonymity to drinking at the bar by yourself, alongside so many others doing the same thing. Their eyes either scanned the televisions that hung high in every corner or burned forward into space. Nobody said anything; nobody was required to.

Thirty minutes before, Andy had tried again to reach out to Beth, only to hear that now-familiar voicemail. "Hi there. It's Beth and Will. Leave a message, and we'll get back to you when we can." Previously, Beth had answered his calls on the first or second ring, her voice lilting with excitement. Now, it seemed she was willing to let him rot, wherever he was.

"You want another beer, Andy?" The bartender, Hank, asked as he stepped up from where he tended to a crossword puzzle.

"Sure thing. Thanks, Hank."

Maybe that was another thing about drinking alone at a bar. The bartender took care of you the way the world didn't. Someone looked out for you when you felt alone the most.

Andy checked his phone to find that he'd missed a call from Beth. The bartender placed the beer before him and collected his empty glass. Andy lifted his phone and tried to call Beth back, only to hit that voicemail all over again. It was a phone tag from hell.

"Andy?"

Andy turned his weary head to find his sister, Claire, and her husband, Russell, who appeared in from the blustery October evening and began to unbutton their coats. Andy's heart sank. The last thing he wanted, right then, was to be wrapped up in conversation with one of his bright and overly chatty sisters.

"What are you up to?" he asked them, trying his darnedest to sound at least half-friendly.

"The girls kicked us out of the living room to watch a movie, so we decided to grab a drink," Claire replied. "Now that they're old enough, we're at a loss for what to do."

"Time to reclaim date nights," Russell added with a vibrant laugh. "Although, to be honest with you, we'll probably sit over in that booth and talk all about Abby's science test and Gail's new obsession with the clarinet."

"You're just obsessed," Andy returned, trying to match their humor.

"Something like that. Hey." Claire's eyes clouded. "I was so sorry to see Beth go the other night. I hope she had at least a bit of fun before she left?"

"Oh, yeah. She was really grateful you girls took her out."

"That's such a relief," Claire returned. "We just love that girl, Andy. Is she meeting you here?"

"Naw. I'm just here to catch up on the game," Andy said as he gestured toward the TV, despite not even fully knowing which game they currently broadcasted. "I still don't have cable set up at my apartment."

"No use doing that now," Claire returned. "Just a few weeks away from your wedding! Gosh, I've been obsessed recently with pairing together floral arrangements for the big day. Charlotte keeps telling me you and Beth want to keep it small. I keep telling her that just because the wedding is small doesn't mean the bouquet has to be. Plus, how many times in your life does your little brother get married?"

Andy's smile faltered. He truly couldn't drum up the strength to have this conversation.

True to form, Claire hardly noticed. The game returned from a commercial break, and Andy feigned interest and shifted his eyes back.

"Okay, then, we'll leave you alone," Claire said hurriedly. "But if the game ends, we'll just be over there. Stop by. Have a drink. Make us feel more interesting than we are."

Andy agreed and turned back toward his beer. How would he tell his family his wedding was off if Beth called it? The worst thing was that maybe they wouldn't be surprised. They'd add it to the already-long list of "ways Andy has failed." Andy half-considered returning to Boston, where he could live out his days alone as planned, without constant reminders of a life he'd yearned for. At least in Boston, he could be empty without judgment.

Andy ordered another drink as the man beside him paid and

But to me, veterans have a unique problem getting back into society afterward. I'm not sure I ever will find a way."

Andy's heart felt shadowed with fear. Clint seemed to translate the heaviness upon his shoulders. He felt that nobody— not even his sisters, his brother nor his parents, or even Beth had ever seen him so clearly.

"I did try the whole marriage thing for a while," Clint continued. "Here on the island. I had two sons and tried my darnedest to raise them the best I could. But they left me, too—all three of them on the same fateful day. My wife said I would never fit into society. Sons resented me for being cruel. Maybe I was. Therapy wasn't exactly a thing you just jumped into back then and I can't say I'm particularly keen even now."

Andy remembered his silly meditation app. Not exactly something he would recommend to a vet like Clint.

"But now, I got my workshop," Clint continued. "And maybe that's all I'll ever need."

Andy's heart stirred with longing. He felt at a loss for words.

A few minutes passed. Andy tried to pay attention to the basketball game but felt nothing. They were flashing images, and an orange ball flung through the air for seemingly no reason at all.

When Clint finished his first drink, he ordered them both another round. With a soft grunt, he added, "You know, you can come by the warehouse again if you want to."

Andy's throat tightened. "I really can't buy anything. As much as I'd love to."

Clint shook his head. "Not about that. Just if you want something to do with your hands during the day. I know how long days can get, especially when you have nowhere else to put your head."

Andy recognized the olive branch.

Maybe this man was the antidote to the next months of uselessness. Maybe he was the answer to the way days piled up, one after another, without rhyme or reason.

"I'll swing by in a few days," he told him. "And I'll try not to let my leg knock me into anything."

Clint grunted with laughter. "Don't worry about your leg, kid. It gets you around just fine."

CHAPTER SIX

BETH HUNCHED her shoulders in the waiting room at the child psychologist's office. A young boy sat on the floor cross-legged with a book wide open on his thighs. He muttered to himself as his mother blinked through tears in the chair beside him. The crumpled Kleenex in her hand reminded Beth of her own early days in this very office when she'd struggled to understand Will's diagnosis and what it would do for their future.

Would her new baby have autism, too?

Was it wrong to hope he or she didn't, since she loved Will with her whole heart and soul? Was it an insult to Will to want a completely healthy baby? No, she was only human after all.

The little boy in the waiting room smashed the book closed, having finished it. His mother nearly jumped from her chair with surprise. Beth didn't react at all, not after the few days she'd spent with Will.

Will had been in conversation with the psychologist, Dr.

continued. "You have to understand that no matter what happens, you have to keep a structure in place for Will. He needs to know that his daily life is manageable. He needs to know what's coming next."

Beth closed her eyes for a moment. Dr. Maverick continued to speak as the world spun around her. She told her everything Beth had read over and over again, in every how-to manual and every blog post about "*How to Raise a Child with Autism.*" When she opened her eyes once more, she found Dr. Maverick still in the midst of what seemed like a never-ending diatribe. Beth thought she might vomit right there and then.

"I'd like to see Will once a week from now on," Dr. Maverick explained. "We had things under control for a good while, but things have shifted. In the meantime, I think it's best that you analyze your situation from all angles and decide what's best for Will. Most especially, he's frightened that he'll have to have a new bedroom somewhere else, that he'll lose the only house he's ever known. And beyond that..." She trailed off for a moment, which left a strange, simmering gap of fear in Beth's stomach.

"What is it?" Beth demanded.

"He's frightened that you'll have a new child. Several of his classmates have said that's what happens when your mother gets remarried. They have a new child— and they no longer care about the one that's left behind."

———

WILL BENT a dutiful head over his novel. Seeing him there, seated in the passenger seat of her car, his eyes scouring the words before him, Beth could half-believe theirs was a world that hadn't shifted at all. She pressed a hand across his forehead and fluttered his hair.

"You want to stop at the store and get some ice cream?"

Will nodded without glancing up from his book. Beth turned on the engine as the first speckles of rain appeared on the windshield. Another dismal autumn afternoon. Another wayward journey through Will's autism.

En route to the store, Andy called again. Will yanked his head up from his book and glared at the phone. Terrified of another meltdown, Beth pressed the "Do Not Answer" button and kept driving as though nothing at all had penetrated their world.

Once at the grocery store, Will grabbed a grocery cart and began to wheel it slowly through the aisles. It was the middle of the day on a weekday, which meant the place was an echo-y ghost town. Beth kept her hand poised just a few inches above Will's shoulder to ensure he had full control of the cart.

"Let's grab some fruits, bud," she told him as she eased them toward the produce section.

"What about ice cream?"

"We'll get that, too."

Beth stuffed apples and pears into baggies as Will took stock of the pumpkin section. They hadn't yet carved a pumpkin for Halloween. Admittedly, Beth had envisioned Andy, Will, and Beth doing that all together in preparation for becoming a fully-formed family. Now, she wasn't sure what to do.

"Would you like to carve a pumpkin this year?" she asked him.

"It's for kids," he told her pointedly, as though he didn't still sleep in train pajamas.

"I'm still a kid at heart," Beth told him. "I'd like to carve a pumpkin."

Together, they picked out two pumpkins. When Beth reached for another, for Andy, Will's face twisted. "We only need two," he said.

It wasn't time to pick a fight. They continued on through the aisles, pausing here and there for cereal boxes and a carton of milk. When they reached the ice cream section, they paused to take stock of the broad array of flavors: strawberry crisp and peanut butter delight and caramel cream. Will inspected every box from outside the glass, making the doors fog up. Beth knew better than to rush him.

That moment, Beth's phone buzzed. She lifted it instinctively to find a text from Andy.

ANDY: Hey. I know things are strange between us right now. I really want to talk.

Beth's knees locked with anxiety. She twitched into the grocery cart, which throttled forward and smacked the doors of the freezer section. Will blinked up, noticed his mother's stricken face, and immediately grabbed her coat. He tugged it as though his life depended on it.

"Mom! Mom! What are you doing? Mom! Pay attention! We're getting ice cream! Mom!"

Beth's nostrils flared with fear as Will's face descended into horror. Tears filled his eyes as a wail sprung up from his throat. Obviously, this meltdown wasn't about the ice cream; it represented something much bigger.

"Baby, it's okay!" Beth bent down, dropping her phone in the process. She took Will's hand and tried to calm him. "Let's just get some ice cream. We'll pay and then go, okay? What about peanut butter chocolate?"

"No! No! No!" Will wailed.

The meltdown continued. Beth's panic mounted to a steady scream in her skull. There seemed to be nothing she could do to calm him. She glanced toward the door, which seemed a million miles away, and waved a hand at one of the grocery store workers, who seemed to want to assist but didn't know how.

Suddenly, out of nowhere came a familiar face.

A pregnant Christine Sheridan stopped her grocery cart only a few feet away. Within this particular cart was a baby carrier, in which Baby Max Sheridan slept on. Christine gave a timid wave and then said, quiet as ever, "Can I help you, Beth?"

Beth nearly collapsed after that. Hurriedly, with the assistance of this beautiful angel, she left the grocery cart where it was, led Will out into the sleeting rain, and fell into her vehicle, snapping Will up in the passenger seat. Back in a familiar space, Will quieted down and burrowed again in his book. Beth let out a low sigh as she pressed her hands against the front of her car.

Christine appeared beside her. She handed her a bottle of water, which Beth drank without a word. After, she closed her eyes and said, "Thank you, Christine. Thank you so much."

"Would you like to come to my house for a while?" Christine asked, stealing a quick glance at Will in the back.

Beth shook her head. "I don't want to take Will anywhere he doesn't know."

"I understand." Christine pondered. "What if I came back with you for a while? We can have a chat?"

Somehow, Christine recognized something within Beth's eyes.

When Christine left an hour later, Beth hugged her tightly, willing herself to say just how thankful she was for her time and her ear. Somehow, exhaustion made her tongue lazy. She couldn't muster the words. All she could do was wave goodbye as Christine eased her car down the driveway, set to return to her family of love and support, while Beth remained alone.

CHAPTER SEVEN

BETH AGREED to meet Andy at the local Oak Bluffs coffee shop after she dropped Will off for his first day at school after his traumatic weekend. Perhaps due to fear, perhaps lack of responsibility, perhaps something else, Andy left five minutes late and barreled into the coffee shop after Beth had already drank half of her cup of tea.

"I'm sorry. I'm so sorry. I know you don't have much time," he apologized empathetically.

Beth rose from her chair, hugged him tenderly, and then sat back down. She remained quiet. Andy turned, ordered a coffee for himself at the counter, then returned to the chair across from her. In Andy's eyes, Beth looked ghastly pale and hollowed out, as though she'd forgotten to eat or sleep for a few days. He noticed that she couldn't stop fidgeting with her hands.

"It's so good to see you," he told her finally. He was reminded of scenes in movies when two people had already broken up but met for a strained conversation after the fact. He and Beth hadn't broken up, not yet. Were they headed there?

"You too." Beth swallowed another gulp of tea.

Andy's coffee arrived. He didn't dare touch it. He wanted to gaze into Beth's gorgeous green eyes for the rest of the time he sat there.

"Did everything go okay dropping Will off?"

Beth shivered. "I don't know. He seemed okay— maybe a bit off, but overall he was fine. He likes his teachers, I guess, and the bullying has quieted down lately."

Andy's heart hammered against his ribcage. "And this past week? Any idea of what triggered all that?"

Beth shook her head slightly, then took a sip of tea and clattered it back in its saucer.

"I've missed you, Beth," Andy admitted then. "I wasn't sure how to help the other day."

Beth's eyes dropped to her cup. "I've missed you, too. I just didn't know how you could help. And I felt with you being there..." She trailed off.

"You felt like it got worse?"

Beth gave a slight shrug. "Yes, maybe a bit. That's not to say Will doesn't love you. He does. He's just a bit... agitated right now. Just yesterday, he had a total meltdown at the grocery store while we were picking out ice cream. Your cousin, Christine, swooped in and helped us out of there. I thought I was going to collapse, but she saved the day, thank God."

Andy's heart felt bruised. Why didn't he know any of this? Why had Beth kept so much from him? He felt he was reading a book without knowing its language.

Beth waved a hand to and fro then said, "But anyway, it's a new day. What have you been up to?"

There she was, side-stepping the conversation at hand. Andy wanted to let her get away with it. He loved her so deeply; he wanted everything to be all right.

"Actually, I'm off to work today," he told her.

Beth's eyes brightened. "No way!"

Andy smiled and leaned back into his chair. "I met this guy the other day when I was running errands with Kelli. He refurbishes old furniture and is restoring an old sailboat in his huge warehouse. It's just him and all these ornate pieces of history. I fell for the place, needless to say, while of course, Kelli managed to put her foot in her mouth."

Beth laughed appreciatively.

"But I met the guy at the bar the other night. He's a vet too, and something of a recluse. We got to talking and he invited me along to show me the ropes. I don't think it's necessarily a common thing he would ask, so I gotta say, I'm both honored and terrified all at the same time. Worried he'll be like, 'Why did I invite this guy to my workshop?'"

"You'll be perfect at this," Beth assured him as her eyes glowed with intrigue.

"I don't know about that, but hey, at thirty-six, I'm not too afraid to try out new things."

After they finished their coffee and tea, Andy paid and led Beth out into the chilly October morning. Beth had to get to the hospital for her shift, and Andy had a date with Clint Isaacson. The rift between the engaged couple felt craggy and enormous. Beth zipped up her jacket but made no move to kiss him. They stood near their

"There he is. Welcome to the workshop. Get on back here and check this out."

Andy's heart, which had hardly beaten at all since Beth's departure from the coffee shop, began to thump wildly in his chest. He eased through the furniture and found himself before a mid-century armoire, which Clint had positioned sideways across the ground to fix up the back. The front of it was incredibly ornate, with brushed golden drawer handles, on which tiny leaves and flowers had been carved out.

"Ain't she a beauty?" Clint asked brightly. "I picked her up at the side of the road outside of Boston, if you can believe it. People just don't care about history anymore. Always want to run to the local superstore to buy the latest thing, which they toss out in another six months."

Andy couldn't help but see the comparison between this mindset and their lives as veterans. They'd done their duty overseas; the United States had "thanked" them the best they could; now, they were left with the aftermath, alone, as though they'd been tossed out.

"Come on. Let me show you some of the other pieces I got going," Clint continued as he removed his gloves and placed them over his worktable. "What's your experience with some of these tools?"

"I have some," Andy offered, remembering his long-ago days working alongside his father, albeit briefly, in his garage workshop, which he'd since closed up. At the time, Trevor had insisted that he wanted his son to know the ropes of "being a man."

"I imagined a man like you had some up his sleeves," Clint told him.

After an initial walk-through of the workshop and warehouse, Clint set Andy up with an antique desk, which had been built between 1912 and 1918 and would probably sell for upwards of two thousand dollars. Clint explained it didn't need as much fine-tuning as the other pieces and was, therefore, a good starting point for old Andy.

As Andy hovered over the desk with his own sanding machine, his brain pulsed with an ever-present worry. How could he possibly grin and converse with this stranger, fine-tune these old pieces, and fight through another day, when even now, Beth spun with thoughts of leaving him behind? But as the silence stretched on, Clint sauntered over to the radio and turned on an oldies tune, which immediately brightened Andy's spirit.

"When I was young, I thought that life was so wonderful," Clint sang. "A miracle, oh, it was beautiful, magical..."

Andy laughed outright at the lyrics to the 1979 Supertramp hit, "The Logical Song."

"That's about damn right," he blared back to Clint, who nodded with finality before he poured himself back over the armoire.

With a final gasp and a lurch of his mind toward pensiveness and concentration, Andy followed Clint's lead. He bent over the antique desk, turned on the sanding machine, and found himself in a simplistic world: just him, the whirr of the machine, and the subtle sanding of a piece of wood with over one hundred years of history behind it. It was his job to carve out space for this desk for the next one hundred years. Nothing else mattered just then.

CHAPTER EIGHT

THAT MORNING, Beth burrowed herself in her work at the rehabilitation clinic at the hospital. She met with a woman who'd recently undergone a stroke, a heart attack victim, a man who'd crashed his car after drunk driving and lived to tell the tale, and a basketball player at the local high school, who said that he frankly couldn't believe his injury might cost him his place on varsity this year. The conversations were varied, and Beth's skillsets flashed out before her beautifully, reminding her, with each instruction she gave, that she had a great deal of purpose on this planet. Why she didn't feel that purpose in her day-to-day life and why she felt so alone these days were questions for another time.

"How's that little guy doing these days?" This was Ellen, one of Beth's only friends and her favorite co-worker, who hovered in the door of the break room fridge as she asked this seemingly playful yet absolutely gutting question.

is speaking out of turn, but I know you've never sat well with your brother..."

Beth's eyes darted up to find Ellen's. A strange rage stirred in the pit of her stomach. Ellen sensed it and snapped her lips together.

"It's just that carrying around guilt for something that happened so long ago isn't going to help anyone. Not Will. Not Andy. And not you," Ellen murmured. "I just wanted to say that."

Perhaps sensing that Beth was on the verge of morphing into a volatile monster, Ellen gripped her glass of orange juice and scuttled out into the hallway. This left Beth to stir in the horror of what she'd just heard as she tried to acknowledge the weight of its truth.

As though to add insult to injury, a half-hour prior to her release from her workday, a familiar, bright, and sunny face appeared at the front desk of the rehabilitation center.

"Beth! I hoped I would run into you." This was Charlotte, Beth's alleged wedding planner, who seemed to swim in endless seas of glorious excitement for anyone's wedding, including Beth and Andy's, which they had said would exist solely within the bounds of Andy's parents' back yard (if it happened at all).

"Charlotte..." Beth tried to conceal her discomfort. "It's good to see you."

"You're off soon, right? The secretary said..."

Beth cast the secretary a disdainful glance. "I sure am."

Charlotte clapped her hands together and fluttered her feet across the floor like an excited child. Beth glanced far down the hallway, trying to drum up an excuse to get her out of whatever Charlotte had up her sleeves.

"We were so disappointed you had to leave the other night," Charlotte told her then. "And I got to talking to Claire earlier this afternoon, and well, we have a surprise for you."

Beth's nostrils flared. How could she push back the resounding love from Andy's family?

"Let me just grab my coat," Beth returned, hoping that their "surprise" was just a little trip to a wine bar or a coffee shop. She would listen to them gab for a while before dismissing herself to pick up Will at four-thirty, after his session with the in-school psychologist.

Beth donned her winter coat, positioned a hat on her head, and wandered into the grey light of the mid-afternoon. Once there, Charlotte honked her horn and eased her car into the drop-off lane. Claire sat in the passenger seat and beckoned for Beth to jump in the back.

Beth buckled herself in and took stock of the back seat of Charlotte's car, which seemed to have exploded with wedding fantasies. Balloons, streamers, cake toppers, fake flowers, a few men's ties, several pairs of socks and women's tights— it all fluttered to and fro between the back seat and the back window.

"Sorry about all that," Charlotte apologized, her eyes scanning the mess. "It's been a whirlwind of weddings since March, I swear. I hardly caught my breath all summer long. And now that it's October..."

"And a full year after that big wedding of yours," Claire interjected.

"Right. I can hardly believe it. But now that it's October, I promised Everett I would slow down a little. Lucky for you and Andy, that means I can piece together a tiny yet beautiful wedding at Mom and Dad's place. And because of all of my connections, I nabbed you a spot with the wedding dress boutique in Edgartown, Something Blue. You must have seen it? It normally has a waiting list about a mile long."

Beth had never even heard of it. She had lost her lust for life the moment her brother, Kurt, had left the world. Now, she felt she'd been kidnapped and forced down the proverbial rabbit hole of "the full wedding experience."

Beth couldn't begin to articulate just how hellish this felt to her. Instead, she sat, listless, in the back, while Charlotte and Claire gabbed endlessly about their daughters, Rachel, Gail, and Abby, who essentially lived their lives as though they were triplets instead of twins and a cousin.

"You've got to be kidding me. That sweater was Rachel's all along? I can't get Gail to wear anything else. It's pretty... hmm..." Claire paused.

"Low-cut? I know. Rachel bought it with spending money she got from Mom. When I saw her in it the first time, I nearly lost my mind," Charlotte returned.

"I mean, what are we going to do? Our girls are growing up so fast. It makes sense they want to dress like it, right?"

"You sound so sensible," Charlotte offered. "But I'm not quite ready for that kind of mature outlook."

Once at the bridal shop, Beth felt sinister and dark as Charlotte illustrated her upcoming wedding to the bridal shop worker with gorgeous words like, "Soul mates, rejoining after years and years apart," and "a small but intimate affair at a private location." Beth thought long and hard about erupting with news of what she'd told Andy just that morning: that she wasn't entirely sure she was ready.

She thought about telling them she'd slept no more than three hours over the past three days.

"A slender bride like you would look incredible in something like this," the bridal shop worker explained as she brought out a long-sleeved ivory-colored gown with a drop waist.

Beth's lips parted in alarm. She hadn't imagined herself looking at anything like this today. It both captivated her and made her want to vomit, all at once. In her high school years, she'd pored over wedding magazines with fanatical zeal. She hadn't assessed the styles of the moment since then.

Yet here it was. And it had the potential to be perfect.

Perfect for another version of Beth, who was allowed to live a very different life.

"Come on! Try it on!" Claire cried.

Beth found herself guided into the dressing room, where she stood center-stage with the dress at hand, which seemed overly heavy for her small frame. She placed the hanger on the hook and spread the fine detail of the fabric out. She wished the younger version of herself could see this— to live in the divine beauty of someone's artistry and craftsmanship, all for the glory of being a bride. Where was that version of Beth? Had she lost all of it?

"Beth? You okay in there?" Claire called out as Charlotte and the bridal shop worker discussed a recent "bridezilla" they'd encountered together, the likes of which they'd never seen before.

"Yep!" Beth's voice rang false as she removed her work clothes and blinked at her naked form in the mirror. The lighting was soft and nourishing, the kind of light you wanted on you when you were almost naked. She supposed this was half the reason brides liked going into this place.

Tenderly, Beth placed her legs into the dress and pulled it up. It hung off of her almost perfectly, highlighting her slender waistline and her porcelain neck. Before she could think twice, the bridal shop worker swung open the curtain, as she had apparently spotted the bottom of the gown beneath the curtain itself.

"Oh my goodness!" Charlotte cried, her hands cupping her mouth.

"Turn around, honey, so we can see you," the bridal shop worker said as she slowly guided Beth around to show her potential sisters-in-law.

"Oh, Beth..." Charlotte's eyes sparkled with tears.

"You look stunning," Claire complimented.

Beth was at a loss. She glanced off to the right, where another few dresses hung on the "sale" rack. These dresses, contrary to the one she now wore, had price tags on them. Each of these "sale" dresses was listed as being over two thousand dollars. Beth's stomach tightened with fear. She was obviously in the wrong boutique.

"I don't even think you should try another one on," Claire cried.

"That's silly. Half the fun is trying on as many as you can," Charlotte insisted. "Beth, I actually saw this other cream one over here... What do you—"

But before Charlotte could finalize her sentence, Beth burst into tears. Her chest heaved with each breath as the bridal shop worker sprung forward to unbutton the gown in the back and release Beth before her salty tears could damage the dress. All the while, Charlotte and Claire looked on; their cheeks turned sallow with shock.

Beth hurried out of the dress and scrambled back into her work clothes. The bridal shop worker muttered to herself as she slipped the dress back onto the hanger. Beth knew she'd embarrassed not only herself but also Claire and Charlotte, both of whom worked in the wedding industry.

When she stepped out of the dressing room, Beth hadn't the strength to look them in the eye.

"I just realized I have to pick Will up from school," she told them softly. "I'll see you both soon. Thank you."

She then hustled out onto the lively streets of an autumn day in Edgartown, where she hailed a cab to whisk her back to the hospital in Oak Bluffs. Perhaps she was the craziest "bridezilla" of all, if only because she wasn't sure if she wanted any of it.

CHAPTER NINE

"HI, ANDY." Kerry Montgomery's voice wavered over the phone ominously. Andy had her on speaker as he drove the rest of the way to the warehouse for his seventh consecutive day with Clint Isaacson. He hadn't communicated much with his family members the previous days and had instead felt his newfound work to be a sort of metaphorical "sanding machine sound" over the rest of the trauma in his life. Beth hardly wanted him; his parents wouldn't understand; he was terrified of what his sisters might think.

But it wasn't like he could just ignore a phone call from his mother.

"Hi, Mom. How's it going?"

"I'm good, honey. Your father's got his crossword going and I'm headed to the book club this afternoon."

Andy allowed a full beat to pass before he answered. "Sounds pretty good."

"You know, your sisters took Beth out the last week."

"I heard about that," Andy returned.

"They seem to think she isn't doing so well. Is Will doing all right? You know, you hear things about people on this island. I can't help but hear gossip. I have these two ears God gave me to listen."

Andy paused at the stoplight and blinked up at it as it swung ominously to-and-fro with the early-November winds.

"Beth's fine, Mom. We're all doing just fine."

The stoplight shifted to green. Andy pressed his foot a bit too hard against the gas and sped through the intersection. Kerry would probably catch wind of that from somewhere later on, as well. "Did you hear your son's been driving recklessly across the island?"

"Charlotte says Beth hasn't even picked out a dress. Are you sure this wedding is still happening?"

Andy's heart thumped. "You know me, Mama. I like to fly by the seat of my pants. We'll let you know when we know. Don't you worry yourself."

"And did Kelli say she'll be the one to marry you? Something about an online wedding certificate..."

Andy and Beth had asked Kelli to perform the ceremony over a month before, back when Beth hadn't purposefully curled away from his touch.

"It's a modern thing, Mom. Not weird or anything. It's just different."

"If you ask me, I think we should have the pastor at least come by. Your father and Uncle Wes are good friends with him. No reason he wouldn't do a brief house call."

Andy couldn't tie himself up with all the details of this now up in the air wedding. He clamped his eyes shut for a split second, then opened them much wider against the horrible brightness of the day.

"I can't really talk about this right now, Mom. Mind if I call you later?"

"What do you have going on? I thought you were still looking for a job. In fact, your father and I would like it if you came by this afternoon to help clean out the garage."

"I can't today, Mom. Let's arrange something for the weekend."

Andy hurriedly told his mother he loved her and ended the phone call. His breath was short, and the pressure on his chest was immense. By the time he reached the parking lot at the warehouse, he was almost in the throngs of a full-scale panic attack.

Back in the workshop, however, he felt a serenity he hadn't thought possible. He was almost finished with the antique desk, which Clint had called "divine" throughout the hours he'd spent on it. "And you probably could guess this about me, but I don't give compliments so easily," Clint had said.

This particular day, Clint spent a number of hours on a large ladder, inspecting the sailboat that hung from the ceiling. Andy remembered that on the first day he'd visited, Clint had said the sailboat was set aside for a very important client. After another round of staining the old desk, Andy stepped toward the boat, lifted his chin, and watched as Clint made a number of notes to himself on a yellow notecard regarding the sailboat and its measurements.

"Need help with anything up there?" Andy called out.

Clint arched one of his thick eyebrows and grunted, "No way, kid. I'm just preparing for a big meet with the client in question."

Axel's face, which seemed to beam with disdain for his father's sincere act of love. Throughout, Andy grappled with the strange dynamic between the two, along with the fact that Clint clearly loved his son to pieces, despite being a crotchety old coot in nearly every other dimension.

After Clint clambered back down from the ladder, he set about grabbing Axel a beer from his mini-fridge. "You in, Andy?" he asked as he dropped down to sift through the multiple beers.

"I have to run, actually," Andy told him. He eyed Axel once more, trying to gauge how much he could trust this horrible, hard-edged man. "But I'll see you in the morning?"

"Sure thing," Clint said, hardly glancing his way. "See you soon."

Will had agreed to stop by Beth's that afternoon to say hello to both her and Will, who had calmed down since his particularly heinous few days the previous week. When Beth had invited Andy, she'd sounded hesitant, as though she wasn't sure she wanted to pair Will and Andy back up again. This frightened Andy more than ever. Will suddenly had the power of his future in his hands.

Andy stopped by a local wine shop to pick up a bottle, grabbed a bouquet of flowers, and soon found himself dusting himself of wood shavings out on Beth's front stoop. It was very like him not to have remembered to pack a change of clothes. Before he could ring the bell, Beth swung open the door to reveal herself, then pressed her finger to her lips to make sure Andy didn't make any loud noises.

"Hi," Andy whispered, again not pleased to have to tip-toe around the concept of Will but grateful, still, to see Beth. He wrapped her up in a hug, and incredibly, she allowed him to hold her for a good while.

"Hi," Beth breathed back before accepting the flowers and stepped back into the house. "It's good to see you. You look... more muscular?"

Andy laughed quietly. "Something about the workshop is good for me, I think."

Beth furrowed her brow as she closed the door. "And you worked out a payment plan with Clint and everything?"

"Yeah. He even promised benefits within the end of the month," Andy continued. "I don't know how I got so lucky."

Beth rolled her eyes playfully, which was the first sign of the "old" Beth he'd seen in ages. "I think it's well-deserved. I can't wait to meet Clint and see the warehouse."

What did this mean? Did this mean that she wanted to marry him again? Did it mean she wanted him in her life? Andy felt swept up in a hurricane of emotion.

"I have another worker bee here, actually," Beth explained as she tiptoed toward the dining room, where they peered in to find Will hard at work on a number of arts and crafts. Under her breath, Beth explained that Will calmed down quite a bit when he had a project like this— that he loved working with his hands and no longer focused on his swirling anxiety.

Andy felt a reflection of himself in these words.

At that moment, Will looked up, caught Andy's eyes, and for whatever reason, actually smiled this time around. "Hi, Andy!" He stood up, ran over to Andy and hugged him tightly.

It was one of the more tender moments Andy had had in quite

a while. Beth looked perplexed. She tilted her head as Will burrowed his head into Andy's chest.

"Should I um... Should I start on dinner?" she asked.

"I think that sounds great," Andy replied brightly. "Maybe Will here can show me the ropes on his crafts?"

"Okay. But you have to be careful with the glue," Will explained as they stepped into the dining room.

Later that evening, as Will, Beth, and Andy continued to glue little seashells onto paper plates in celebration of Will's enormous seashell collection, Andy suggested that Will check out his "arts and crafts" the following afternoon after school. Beth immediately stiffened. She gave him a bug-eyed look.

"I don't know about that..."

But Will nodded and furrowed his brow. "I would like to see something like that. Adult arts and crafts. Maybe that's something I would really like." He then returned to the work-at-hand as his glasses slipped lower down his nose.

Andy's eyes met Beth's. She gestured out toward the kitchen then got up in expectation of Andy following her. When they reached the kitchen, she whispered, "I still don't know. He's been all over the place lately. I don't want something to set him off."

"Come on, Beth. Let's just see how tonight goes. We'll sit together. Hang out. And if all goes well, I'll pick him up at school tomorrow and bring him to the workshop. It'll be after-hours, so it's not like any of the machines will be on. Safety first and all that."

Beth heaved a sigh. It was difficult to read her facial expression.

"Beth, I know you've been burning the candle at both ends," Andy continued. "And I feel like you haven't let me help you with any of it. Just let me support you, just for the afternoon. And maybe that support will lead to even more support as time goes by. What do you think? Besides, Beth, even if you don't marry me in a few weeks— I already feel like we're a family. Me, you and Will. The rest of my family can be a lot. I know that. Heck, I ran away from them for nearly twenty years. But this is you and me, Beth. We've been good since we met. Let's keep this going. We owe it to ourselves."

daughter about sex" thing and had also instilled fear in Beth regarding anything relating to the subject. Beth hadn't been with many men, especially in the wake of her brother's death. Things had changed that summer. Now, it seemed, times would never return to the way things had been.

As the doctor asked Beth a number of questions regarding her sexual history and her potential for this pregnancy, a portion of Beth's mind set aside space to consider what the heck she'd been thinking during June, July, and August. She'd fallen head-over-heels with a stranger who'd allowed her to forget, if only for a moment, that her parents had pushed her far away after her brother's death. That was no excuse to bring a human into this world of pain and cruelty.

The doctor investigated and found that, yes, in fact, she was six weeks pregnant.

For six weeks, Beth Leopold actually hadn't been alone. Those nights she'd cried herself to sleep, she'd cradled a collection of cells within her, proof that she'd had a form of love, at least— a version she'd been able to cling to until he'd departed the island.

"What about the father?" the doctor asked her now. "Any contact?"

"Not at all," Beth told her as her voice cracked.

"You do have options," the doctor informed her. "I'll give you these pamphlets. We can meet next week to discuss them further."

Beth had moved into a tiny apartment at the age of twenty-two but still returned to her parents' house frequently to check in. Almost instinctively, she drove back now and parked in the driveway, willing time to draw itself backward and cast her into her teenage years again, when Kurt had been alive. As she paused in the driveway with the engine off, her mother stepped outside to water a mum in its hanger. Beth stepped out of the car to meet her mother's gaze.

"Are you going to come inside? Or do you plan on sitting out there all afternoon?"

Beth had washed clean after last night's party, which, at the time, had seemed like her last hurrah (without alcohol, of course). Even still, she felt as though her mother sensed the "party" on her. She eyed her with a penetrating gaze and asked her questions about her job at the hospital and her wayward summer of beaches and sailboats and "rich men." Gossip traveled fast across the island; Beth knew better than to act the way she had.

"Gosh, if only your brother were here," her mother said now as she poured them each a cup of tea.

Beth could have counted on both hands the number of times she'd heard her mother say that over the past few weeks. It seemed to be her favorite refrain.

"I just can't understand how anyone could still uphold that mission..." Mrs. Leopold continued. "And Andy Montgomery's still over there, for some reason."

"Mom?"

"We buried his best friend, and then he just keeps going, fighting a battle that Kurt can't even believe in any longer," Mrs. Leopold continued. "It just turns my stomach."

"Mom, can I please tell you something?"

Mrs. Leopold slurped her tea and placed the cup back in its saucer. "What's up, honey?" she blurted with impatience, willing Beth to hurry up.

"I have some news," Beth whispered. She dared herself to keep her eyes wide open— dared herself to keep her mother's gaze. "I learned that, well... I'm pregnant."

The shock radiated across her mother's face as her chin quivered. She made no motion to smile. About thirty seconds passed, maybe more, before Beth asked, "Will you please say something?"

"Tell me what I'm supposed to say, Beth."

Beth's heart dropped. She stared at her hands, no longer willing to look her mother in the eye. "I don't want you to say anything you don't want to say."

"That's right. You wouldn't want me to lie," her mother continued. "You wouldn't want me to say that this will taint an already broken family. You wouldn't want me to say that I didn't see this coming, with you running all over the island with those men from the city."

Beth yearned to curl up into a ball and die. She shivered with fear.

"I just can't imagine why you want to break this already broken family more," her mother continued.

"I don't see how a baby can cause any of this negativity..." Beth told her. "I don't see a baby being anything less than a blessing..."

"Come on, Beth. Grow up already," her mother blared.

Beth couldn't listen to this any longer. She rushed to her feet and ran for the door as her mother cried out, "Your brother would have stopped you from hanging around those men! He would never have let this happen. Never!"

PRESENT

IT HAD BEEN ten years since Beth Leopold had sat in the waiting room of the gynecologist with a secret in her belly. Remarkably, they hadn't updated the decor much, if at all, and even the chairs were that same sticky material, the likes of which reminded you, no matter what, that you were in a doctor's office and things were probably about to change forever. It wasn't like they let you sit in a comfy chair as you learned about your next profound step in life.

The same doctor from ten years before performed the same test and informed her that, yes, this time she was eight weeks pregnant — calling it "a truly exciting time." Beth asked all the relevant questions as a tear rolled down her cheek. A baby. A baby, now, as everything else shifted. Was her family up for this? Was she?

As she walked back into the lobby, she flashed through a number of future images: Will, mid-freak-out, as she tried to change the diaper of a screaming baby. Will panicked as the baby interrupted his perfectly outlined schedule. Will, hating the baby with all the strength he had, just because she or he had come into his world like a bomb.

It was now early November and the skies told a story of the harrowing, dark winter that awaited them. Beth bundled herself up near the door, nestling her nose beneath a scarf in preparation for her walk back to her car. Will had probably been at the warehouse with Andy for a good hour or so, and Beth had a real itch to rush over and make sure everything was all right.

"Beth?" The voice rang out through the howling of the wind.

Beth walked around to witness Kelli Montgomery, and her black trench coat whipped out behind her as she neared the door.

CHAPTER ELEVEN

ANDY DOUBLE-CHECKED Will's seatbelt as his ears rang with a jolt of panic. Will paid no attention to his manic expression as his eyes scanned from the latched belt to the cross-over to Will's tennis shoes, planted firmly on the backseat of Andy's car. Will had already burrowed his nose into a book and begun to mutter the first words to himself. Andy started the engine and immediately turned down the music to zero. This was Will's territory and he wasn't about to mess it up.

Andy had spoken to Clint about the arrangement earlier that morning. Since Axel's trek back to the Vineyard, Clint seemed in an endless array of various moods. One moment, he whistled atop the ladder, sandpaper in hand and the next, he clunked his fist against the worktable and bruised the inside of his hand. When he learned about Will and his upcoming visit, he simply grunted and said, "If you think you can handle having a son around." Five minutes later, he countered that with, "I'll run out to the store and get some snacks."

When Will and Andy pulled up outside of the warehouse, Will closed his book dutifully, slipped it back in his backpack, and gazed out the window at the enormous building. So far, not a tantrum in sight. His teacher had even mentioned that Will was incredibly calm today. She'd even used the term "go with the flow," which was nothing Andy had ever heard associated with Will.

Andy guided Will into the workshop, a kind of wonderland of fascinating smells and shiny machines and ornate furnishings from across time and space. The strange luminescent light glittered strangely across Will's glasses as he lifted his chin to inspect the sailboat on high.

"Wow," he breathed.

"Is that our visitor?" Luckily, Clint seemed to display a rather good mood. He sauntered around the refurbished piano, something of a newfound hobby for Clint, then bent down to stick out a hand to shake Will's.

Will's eyes widened as this large man overtook him. Andy prayed he would recognize Clint as nothing more than an old man.

"Pleased to meet you," Will recited formally. "My name is Will. Will Leopold."

"And my name is Clint Isaacson," Clint told him as they shook hands slowly. "I'd like to welcome you to my workshop. Your friend Andy and I work here every day together, fixing old antiques and the like. Andy tells me you like old things. Like dinosaurs."

"Dinosaurs are much older than these furnishings," Will informed him. "Millions of years older."

"I don't think we can compete with that. But fifty? A hundred? A little bit more? That's more our scene," Clint explained.

Slightly frightened but willing to hang, Will slipped his hand into Andy's as Clint guided them through the massive warehouse, explaining the various techniques they used to return items to their former glory. Will asked several questions that indicated that he'd researched the industry the night before, maybe after Andy had already left Beth's for the night. Andy again faced the innermost hope within his heart: that one day soon, he would be allowed to stay up with Will and discuss his various loves and obsessions, digging into new worlds together in a way that united them.

"And this, Will is a sailboat I plan to build back up for my son," Clint explained as he stretched a long, muscular arm up toward the hanging, ragged beauty.

Will's eyes widened. "It's very busted."

"Yes. That's true. It requires a whole lot of work," Clint told him patiently. "But you know what? I think I have the dedication to make it happen."

That moment, the front door of the warehouse flung open to reveal Axel Isaacson. Yet again, he was dressed in an immaculate suit, which seemed to broaden his shoulders all the more, along with a pair of aviator sunglasses and shining shoes of Italian leather. He paused at the sight of his father with this younger child but didn't bother to smile, the way nearly every other man or woman might have on the Vineyard.

"Axel! I didn't know you planned to drop by this afternoon," Clint remarked.

Axel grunted hello and continued to blink down at Will. He

the antique mirror section, with the lithe ease of a ballerina. When she found Will, she collected him within her thin arms and held him tightly as his eyes closed and his cries softened. Beth was Will's home in every regard. She'd reminded him of solid ground.

Will slowly returned to himself. Quietness hung heavy over them like winter clouds. Clint disappeared and then returned with a wide selection of snacks, including juice boxes, fruit snacks, crackers, and cheese. He arranged them out on a plate and beckoned for Will to approach the worktable. Beth held Will's hand and guided him toward the station, where Will sat on the edge of a stool with his legs swinging back and forth as he assessed the food before him.

Everyone— including Axel Isaacson breathed a collective sigh of relief.

"Thank you so much," Beth said as she lifted her eyes toward Clint, whom she hadn't met before. "I'm Beth, by the way. I guess you've already met my son, Will."

Clint stretched out a hand to shake hers. Beth's smile was luminescent. Andy felt himself fall in love with her all over again— this bright and shining woman in the midst of a confusing world.

"It's good to meet you. Andy's told me lots about you," Clint offered.

"All good, I hope," Beth returned.

She then turned her face around to greet Axel. Andy knew the greeting wouldn't go well and assumed Axel would leave her with a disgruntled comment and an annoyed flip of his head, as he had with Andy.

But instead, as Andy followed Beth's eyes toward Axel, he witnessed a very different expression.

In fact, Axel looked at Beth now as though she were a ghost.

When Andy traced his eyes back toward Beth, she reflected a similar expression.

It was very clear that the two of them had met before.

Andy's heart thumped then flipped over. All the color drained from Beth's cheeks. Axel cleared his throat as Will lifted his juice box, stabbed the straw inside, and began to slurp up the over-sugared liquid.

"Beth?" Axel spoke first, using a very different tone than he had even five minutes before. It was softer, similar to the way Andy spoke to Beth when they were alone.

Beth slid a strand of hair behind her ear nervously.

"I guess you two know each other?" Clint looked between the two of them.

Nobody spoke. Silence, save for the crunch of Will's teeth over his snacks, permeated through the air. Andy felt he'd never heard a more devastating silence.

Finally, Axel turned his gaze toward Will, whose eyes were a dramatic blue, the color of the Vineyard Sound itself. When Andy glanced back at Axel's eyes, he recognized the same color— a perfect match.

"Oh my God," Axel exclaimed finally, articulating the same thought everyone in that room had at once. "Look at him."

CHAPTER TWELVE

THERE THEY WERE: the bright, penetrating ocean-colored eyes that continued to haunt Beth in her dreams many years after she'd last witnessed them. Remarkably, she had discovered them again, in a place beyond her wildest dreams: the antique warehouse in which her fiancé now worked. Between them sat her son, Will, mid-way through a crunchy, salty pretzel, peering up at a man she'd never in a million years assumed he would meet.

"I'm sorry," Beth said then, fumbling over her words. "I think Will and I should head back home. This has obviously been too much for him." She used the tone she so often used when it came to Will: one of formality and hope that everything else would be forgiven. She collected Will's free hand in hers, bent down again, and whispered in her sweetest, most loving voice, "You want to head home now? We can watch that documentary about the dinosaurs all over again if you want to." Will had begged for the movie all week long as Beth had insisted on other modes of play, if

years ago since then, as she'd purposefully left those memories behind.

Now, she propped herself up against the wall of the hallway with her legs stretched out in front of her. Within the bath, Will splashed around and sang little songs to himself. Beth slowly opened the photo album to the early-summer snapshots, in which she and her girlfriends had posed in bikinis, drinking red bubbly alcoholic drinks as the sun sunk into the ocean behind them. There was such bliss on her face, the likes of which hadn't been spotted in any mirror sense. Motherhood did that to you: cratered your face and took some of the optimism from your eyes.

She continued to flip as the memories raced through her mind: meeting Axel Isaacson at a beach party near Edgartown as the light had dimmed around them. Her whispering, "Isn't he cute?" to a nearby girlfriend. The memory of him bringing her a beer and complimenting her miniskirt; her drinking the first one and then three more before falling into him, giggling madly. He then put his hand across the small of her back and kissed her as the moon grew pregnant in the night sky.

The first photo taken of Beth and Axel was from the Fourth of July, approximately three weeks after they had met. In it, Axel had his thick arms wrapped around the small of Beth's waist. Beth's smile was electric, the kind you only saw in old photographs of people whose lives had gone very wrong just afterward. On one of those nights around the Fourth of July, Beth had told Axel for the first time about her brother's death, and he'd held her while she'd cried out drunken tears before falling asleep in the front of his car. She'd loved him, maybe, but only in the silly way you loved summer affairs. Not that she'd had that many. He'd been the only man of her early mid-twenties. She'd never had time to ask herself if that was a sad thing.

Axel had mentioned a father he didn't like very much. Had he said the father was the reason he was on the island in the first place? Beth couldn't remember. Her memories of Axel were buried beneath all her glowing (and traumatic) memories of having Will. Her memories raced back to when Will, blinked up at her in the hospital bed or when he wrapped his entire hand around her little finger, then a flash of Will, taking his first steps and stomping off to the other side of the room before falling to his padded bum wrapped in a diaper.

Axel was never meant to come into the equation. He'd been a blip that had led to the rest of her and Will's life.

Now, somehow, he'd discovered her.

Between the run-in with Kelli that afternoon and the horrific discovery of Will's father at Andy's warehouse, Beth wasn't sure how much of any of this she could attribute to bad luck. Was she just a bad person?

She closed the photo album again and listened to the soft sounds of Will playing in the bath. Her right hand extended over her belly as she closed her eyes, trying to communicate with the baby within.

The man she'd just witnessed had nothing at all to do with her and Will and Andy. He'd been a donor of sperm, in every sense of the word and that was it.

But now that he had discovered them. Would he want something from them? Would he demand some kind of information from them? Would he work to tear through the beautiful facade she'd crafted for them and rip them out of their comfort zone even more than they already were?

The thought terrified her.

"Mom? I'm ready."

Beth stood up from the floor, placed the photo album on the foyer table, and headed into the bathroom with a large fuzzy towel extended on either side. Will stepped into it and allowed his hair to be rubbed and his shoulders to be patted before he took on drying responsibilities himself. Beth then followed him to his bedroom, where he slipped on his pajamas and slipped himself under the comforter.

"Will you say a prayer, William Leopold?" she asked him gently.

Will nodded as the lights dimmed in his eyes. "I will. By myself."

Beth nodded. "Good night, baby. I love you."

"I love you, too."

Beth clipped the door shut and hovered outside for a moment, listening to Will as he spoke his prayers delicately. He made sure to thank God for Andy, "one of the best guys in the world."

CHAPTER THIRTEEN

AFTER BETH'S DRAMATIC DEPARTURE, Andy called her several times to check-in, but it only went to voicemail. He hovered in the rain outside of the warehouse as Axel and Clint tore through a heavy discussion inside. Although Andy burned with curiosity about what they said, Clint had asked him for a moment of privacy, and Andy had known better not to resist. Now, Axel burst from the warehouse doors and strutted through the rain toward his BMW. He walked past Andy as though he wasn't there at all.

Andy returned to the belly of the warehouse, where he found Clint again at the top of the ladder, which teetered beneath him slightly. The radio spit out oldies, just as it always had, as though time itself hadn't just stopped short in its tracks. Clint made a small note on his yellow pad regarding the sailboat, pursed his lips together, and whistled like a songbird.

"Clint?" Andy felt suddenly like a much younger, much more

toward the hallway to display her ridiculous Jack-o-Lantern sweater. Her smile flickered slightly when she saw only Andy. "There he is. My handsome son!" She rushed for him and planted a kiss on his cheek.

"Beth and Will couldn't make it," Andy explained softly. "Not feeling well."

"Oh, that's too bad," Kerry offered as she latched a hand around Andy's elbow and led him into the dining room. "Everyone! Andy's here."

From the doorway, Andy took full stock of his family. Claire sat alongside Russell while their twin girls, Gail and Abby, tore through their pre-dinner biscuits with the zeal of hungry teenage girls. Beside them, Charlotte's daughter, Rachel, seemed to text under the table. Probably, she was about two seconds from getting caught for it. Her mother, Charlotte, along with Charlotte's boyfriend, Everett, took up the rest of that side of the table while Steven and his son Jonathon sat across from them. Kelli and her daughter, Lexi, sat in heavy discussion about the boutique, which Lexi had begun to operate almost full-time while doing online business classes. Andy's father, Trevor, had his familiar place at the head of the table while Kerry bustled around, grabbing an extra chair from the living room and placing it between Kelli and their father.

"There he is," his father boomed as Andy sat. "How're things at the warehouse? Kelli here told me all about it."

Kelli's cheek twitched. "Can't believe you work with that guy every day."

"He's not as bad as he seemed that day," Andy offered. His cheeks flushed with embarrassment immediately afterward. He had to stand up for Clint. Just now, Clint felt like one of his only friends in the world. "Actually, he's pretty incredible. He started the warehouse all by himself and has a real way with the antiques. He's already taught me a lot."

Trevor's eyes were difficult to read: shadowed and far away. "You remember when I used to teach you a thing or two in my workshop?"

Of course, Trevor Montgomery needed to draw the conversation back to something he understood. Perhaps all people were like that: uninterested in your stories unless they were somehow involved.

"I sure do. Gave me a good base," Andy told him, knowing he had to.

Kerry called Steven into the kitchen to carry the heavy chicken alfredo dish, which he positioned at the center of the table, alongside the green beans and the mashed potatoes. Charlotte rose to uncork another bottle of wine. With a flourish, she retrieved another glass from the armoire, filled it, then placed it in front of Andy.

"We got a head start on you, baby brother," she told him with a wink.

The mood was overwrought with electricity and life. Andy couldn't help but contrast it to the own darkness within his soul. Had it been a mistake to come? No, he thought to himself. At least this was a good distraction. It was nourishing food. It was listening to Rachel, Gail, and Abby rehearse their Shakespearean play, in which Gail played one of the leads. It was his mother leaping up every few minutes to grab another spoon or another knife or another thing of sauce. The swirling chaos of it all was the direct antithesis of Andy's sallow little apartment.

"Have you started your move-in to Beth's yet?" Steven asked during a lull in the conversation.

Andy stabbed his fork into his mashed potatoes. "Not quite, but it's not like I have much stuff. It won't take me too long."

"So you are moving in soon?" Claire asked brightly. She picked at her green beans and turned her eyes toward Charlotte. "We just saw Beth the other day. She's such a lovely girl."

"Yes, but really pushing her luck as far as dresses go!" Charlotte, whose entire world revolved around weddings, returned.

"She looked just beautiful. Even the store clerk said so," Claire countered.

"What do you mean?" Andy asked, completely perplexed by his sister's comments.

"Oh, we learned she didn't have a wedding dress yet, and we took her out," Claire replied like it was no big deal.

"I refuse to let my future sister-in-law get married in a paper bag," Charlotte returned. "But she's really pushing her luck."

Kelli had been incredibly quiet thus far throughout dinner. Now, she turned her head just the slightest bit to catch Andy's gaze.

"Where is Beth tonight, anyway?" She shared no smile.

"She's not feeling well," Andy replied as he pushed his food around on his plate, deep in thought.

"I see." Kelli dropped her eyes back to her plate. Her expression seemed loaded.

"I'm sure if we grab something in the next week or so, we'll be all right," Charlotte continued.

"And we're still having it here?" Kerry asked as she turned out toward the back porch, her face shadowed with doubt. "Oh my, just looked at the yard. I should really have a landscaper come by and tend to the backyard before the wedding pictures. And you really think it's okay to have Kelli perform the ceremony?" The wrinkles between her eyebrows deepened.

"We can always push the wedding to next year," Charlotte continued. "If you'd actually like to put something together. I've asked Beth over and over again to tell me her wedding wishes. I've never met a girl without at least one or two!"

"She's had a lot on her plate over the years," Steven countered before he sipped his wine.

Kelli dropped her chin lower to her chest. Her cheeks had turned a strange green color. Andy leaned toward her ear and whispered, "Hey! Are you doing okay?"

Kelli nodded but quickly grabbed her napkin and pressed it over her lips. She erupted from her chair so quickly that it clattered to the ground.

"Oh my gosh! Kelli?" Claire did a half-jump from her chair.

"Don't worry about me. Something went down the wrong pipe!" Kelli called back.

But Andy sensed something was wrong. Claire returned to her seat and continued to gossip with Charlotte as Andy rose up and followed Kelli into the kitchen. There, he found her gripping either side of the sink, staring at the little slices of vegetables alongside the bubbles that lined the metal belly.

"Kelli? Are you okay?"

Kelli bit down on her lower lip. Andy's heart stirred with sorrow. He'd always felt they could tell one another everything.

"Did something happen with Xander?"

Kelli shook her head. "No. Xander's great. Everything's great."

"I know you well enough to know you're lying."

Kelli laughed ominously. She turned her eyes to meet Andy's. They held each other's gaze for a long, stark moment. "You don't have to get all swept up in that wedding stuff, you know. It seems like Beth isn't."

Andy's nostrils flared.

"What is that suppose you mean?"

Kelli grabbed a napkin and fluttered it beneath her eyes. "I just hope you watch out for yourself in all of this. My biggest regret was not taking care of myself as I got closer to Mike. Beth is a wonderful person. But wonderful people can do just as much damage as others — sometimes more, because I think we trust that they won't hurt us."

Andy squinted at his sister, confused at what she was trying to say. His lower lip quivered just slightly. He suddenly felt a great distance between himself and Kelli. Perhaps in another dimension, he might have told her about the strange incident at the warehouse. But here and now, Kelli was painting a picture of Beth that he really didn't like.

"Anyway, let's get back to dinner," Kelli breathed then as she stepped past him and headed into the dining room.

"You doing okay, honey?" Charlotte called as Kelli joined them.

"I think I'll make it out alive," Kelli countered. "As long as I don't eat too much of Mom's cheesecake."

Andy remained in the kitchen. His legs felt as heavy as lead. Outside, several splatters of rain had given over to sleet and snow. Without a word, he headed back toward the front closet, where he collected his coat and hat and retreated from the warmth of his family. Yet again, he felt like a foreigner in a strange land where he couldn't speak the language. He wanted to sit in the shadows of himself, all alone.

CHAPTER FOURTEEN

WILL WASN'T UP for school the following morning. Beth called into work and stood listless at the kitchen counter in her robe as coffee dripped into the pot. Will clicked his train tracks together in the living room, still in his train pajamas, lording over a world he could understand. Beth drummed up the bravery to text Andy back, knowing her avoidance of the situation would only make it heavier on both of them.

BETH: Hey. I'm sorry I left like that.

BETH: Maybe we can talk about it when you get off of work if you have time.

Andy texted back immediately, as though he had watched his phone with obsessive fear.

ANDY: I told Kelli I'd help her with something at the Overlook after I'm finished at the warehouse. Maybe after? I could stop by in the evening? If you're up for it.

Will made soft "zooming" noises as he pushed a train over its tracks, casting it out on a wild journey from the couch to the television. When she'd tried to get him ready for school that morning, he'd thrown a train across his bedroom. A dark gash over the sterling white paint told the story of a chaotic boy with spinning thoughts she couldn't possibly understand.

The doorbell rang then, but Beth ignored it initially. Normally, she wouldn't have been home at this hour, and she wasn't keen on spontaneous house calls, as they disrupted her and Will's schedule. But after the bell rang two more times, Will lifted his head and asked, "Are you going to get that, or should I?"

Beth padded into the foyer to find a familiar figure peering through the little top window of the door. Kelli Montgomery, the soon to be sister in law who now held one of her dearest secrets.

"Hello, Kelli."

Kelli's lips were incapable of smiling. She wore a thick trench coat that gleamed with Vineyard rain.

"I don't mean to just drop in on you like this," Kelli began.

Actually, she did mean to do that, Beth thought. That was precisely what she'd done.

"I just wanted to tell you that I saw Andy last night and I found it very difficult to hold onto this secret, especially because he's suffering right now. I don't know what's going on with the two of you. I just know that I don't like seeing my brother like this. He's been through enough."

Beth's stomach felt hollow and strange. She gaped at this woman as the weight of her problems seemed to double. As she stuttered, searching for any kind of answer, another vehicle appeared in the driveway, slotting itself in behind Kelli's. An unfamiliar man appeared. He carried a large brown envelope beneath his arm as he sauntered toward them with an air of importance.

Kelli followed Beth's gaze to ogle this new visitor. Her lips parted in surprise.

"Good morning. Are you Beth Leopold?" the man asked in a formal tone.

"I am."

He passed her the envelope and instructed her to open it. "I've been instructed to ensure you read the contents of this envelope."

Beth's arm shook so violently that she nearly dropped the envelope to the ground. Kelli sidled up to face the unfamiliar man.

"Who are you?" Kelli demanded.

"I represent the legal interests of Axel Isaacson," the man responded simply.

"And who the heck is Axel Isaacson, exactly?" Kelli demanded.

Beth felt terribly cold. Slowly, she slid out the documents within the envelope, in which a member of Axel's legal team had crafted a signed document that demanded a DNA test for her son, Will, regarding paternity.

Beth's jaw dropped as she scanned the document.

It has come to Axel Isaacson's attention that Will Leopold may be his rightful heir. Throughout his young life, he's developed a number of emotional problems, which very well could have been avoided had the boy known his father. If Axel Isaacson is found to be Will Leopold's father, legal consequences will follow.

"Beth? Beth? Can you hear me?" Kelli asked under her breath, as she couldn't read the letter from where she stood.

the picture she'd drawn up for the both of them and demanding space.

"I don't want to put Will through any stupid paternity test," she muttered.

Kelli nodded. "You've done all this yourself. It seems insane that he should demand anything of you."

Beth's stomach curdled strangely. She jumped up from her chair and hustled to the bathroom as the world around her faded. She crumpled over the toilet as the first round of this baby's morning sickness took hold of her at the very worst time. The sound of it rattled from wall to wall.

When she was finished, Beth mopped up her face best she could but still found a blotchy-eyed stranger peering back in the mirror. Back in the kitchen, she found Kelli pouring her another cup of tea and talking on the phone.

"Don't mean to step on your toes, but this is kind of an emergency," Kelli explained in soft tones. "If you could fit us in before lunch, that would be incredible. Okay. Thank you. See you soon."

Kelli urged Beth to take a shower. Beth's limbs felt like weights. She stood, defeated, as sharp lines of hot liquid dragged over her back. When she left the bathroom, she found Will all dressed in his favorite outfit: purple pants with a yellow sweater. The pairing was enough to make anyone laugh aloud, but Will adored it.

"Kelli says we're going out," Will explained.

Kelli reappeared with her coat on. "I know we Sheridan-Montgomery people can be a bit overwhelming. But we've got a lawyer to back us up."

Kelli drove Beth and Will to the downtown law offices of

Sheridan and Sheridan, which Susan Sheridan had opened with her daughter, Amanda, the previous spring. Susan had worked as a criminal lawyer in Newark alongside her ex-husband, Richard, for over twenty years. She'd moved to the island to work at the Sunrise Cove Inn but had soon found her mind stuffed to the gills with towel inventories and guest complaints. Her world was the legal world— and she'd built a new one for herself on the island.

Amanda Harris, Susan's daughter, appeared in the foyer to greet them. Her cousin, Audrey, happened to be in the foyer with her son, Max. Audrey wore a Penn State University sweatshirt.

"Hi! Mom said you were stopping by," Amanda said. "She's just finishing up a meeting." She then bent down toward Will and said, "You remember me, Will? You want to hang out with us for a while?"

"We're not so bad, Will," Audrey offered brightly. "Maybe a little more boring than we used to be, but..."

"It's okay. I brought my book," Will told them as he slid into one of the waiting room chairs and burrowed himself away.

That moment, Bruce, Susan's newest partner, stepped out of Susan's office. He greeted them warmly and gestured back toward Susan, who scrawled a note to herself on a pad of paper.

"She's all ready for you," he told them.

Susan took Beth's envelope, removed the papers swiftly, and read the letter from Axel's lawyer with squinted eyes. When she reached the end, she exhaled all the air from her lungs.

"His lawyer is Jack Froth," she said under her breath.

"Who's that?" Kelli demanded.

Susan twirled her fingers through her lush brunette locks, which had grown back in after the previous year's bout with breast cancer. It seemed remarkable to Beth that Susan could tread through the depths of death with such bravery and come back on top like this. Beth didn't have that kind of strength.

"He's one of the best lawyers in New York City," Susan offered. "Not exactly the kind to mess with."

"What does that mean?" Beth found her voice.

"It means that even if you fight this, Jack Froth will probably find a way to force your hand toward a paternity test," Susan said. "It would mean a lot of court dates and a whole lot of messiness."

"That's ridiculous," Kelli returned. "Beth's raised Will since day one. What right can this guy possibly have?"

"It's not entirely fair. I agree," Susan affirmed. "But again, if he has money to throw around, he could push this pretty far." Her eyes widened to the size of saucers. "I'm so sorry, Beth. The best way through this is to go ahead with the test. I can help you through whatever I can. But it seems like you've fallen into a big pit of bad luck."

CHAPTER FIFTEEN

DENISE WAS off the island for a trip to Washington D.C., which left Beth's hands tied with regards to babysitting options. As a last-ditch effort, she called Ellen, who nearly screeched with joy. "I told you if you ever need me to watch Will, I'll do it. You don't use me enough, I swear." Beth's heart glowed with the enormity of this woman's friendship and the leaps and bounds Susan and Kelli had performed for her only that morning. Throughout the fright of this coming hurricane, she had to learn to hold onto people for support. It was the only way she would survive.

With Andy at the Aquinnah Cliffside Overlook Hotel for the rest of the early evening, Beth drove the opposite direction toward Clint Isaacson's warehouse. For a long moment, she hovered in the doorway of the old smoggy place, inhaling the dense wood-tinged air. Clint's radio spit out an old Styx tune, one her father had loved. It was strange the way music could pull you through time and space, directly to a memory you didn't know you had.

always gets his way. He built up millions of dollars over the previous eight years because he's ruthless in all areas of his life."

Clint stepped away from his worktable and lifted his chin to gaze up at the hanging sailboat. His shoulders fell back.

"I really thought this stupid boat would bring the two of us together," he said softly. "Thought it would be a way forward for the two of us. I wanted to prove myself as some kind of man. A man he might want to keep around. A man he might want to get to know. But he's been increasingly hard— difficult. Probably, he's a direct reflection of myself— hard and stoic and difficult to get along with. I bet he's giving me a dose of my own medicine." Clint laughed outright, then added, "And now, he's giving that medicine to you, too."

"I never wanted any trouble," Beth told him pointedly. "I never needed anyone else."

Clint's chuckle was almost unkind. "That's where you're wrong. Throughout all my years of loneliness, I told myself the same thing; that I never needed anyone and that I was alone on this earth for a reason. But the minute I meet someone who reminds me of kindness and compassion and love..." He whacked himself in the thigh. "That's when I realize what an idiot I've been all these years to siphon myself off from the rest of humanity."

Beth took a small step back. Her hip skidded against the edge of a secretary desk, which hobbled around. Clint made no motion to scold her, as he was too lost in his own thoughts.

"Maybe I was foolish to think I ever could have mended that," Clint said then, speaking both of his relationship with his son and the boat which hung in the warehouse. "Maybe I should just let it go."

Beth closed her eyes as a tear ran down her cheek. When she opened her eyes again, she found Clint peering at her across the old furniture.

"He's staying on the south side of Edgartown. The cul-de-sac at the end of Pleasant Ave. Massive house. You can't miss it."

Beth wasn't sure she would ever have the bravery to actually go to this mansion and speak to this stranger with plans to ruin her life.

"But just to be clear," Clint added. "He feels his entire life exploded in his face. And I don't doubt he feels it's his right to ruin anyone else's life around him, just because he can."

CHAPTER SIXTEEN

ELLEN: **Don't worry about us. We've got a movie picked out and pizza on the way.**

> **ELLEN: Just do your thing, babe!**

Beth pressed her phone against her chest as she pondered what to do next. Out in the world without a plan and without a Will, she felt at a loss, cast into the swirling seas of other people's plans for her future. She'd texted Ellen to make sure everything was all right at home, and with her response, she was allowed to do the thing she hadn't allowed herself to do in what seemed like ages.

She wanted to run into the arms of the man she loved so much. She wanted to be held. She wanted to be told everything would be all right, even if it wasn't.

Beth drove the familiar route out to the Aquinnah Cliffside Overlook Hotel. In August, Andy had actually proposed on the beach below the cliffs, dropping on one knee and looking at her with those impossibly beautiful eyes. "I can't imagine doing any of

over some good food. I have to guess you haven't eaten much since you found out."

Beth's laugh was ironic. Food hadn't crossed her mind once.

"I'd like that."

They decided to leave Beth's car at the cliffs to be picked up later. This allowed Beth to sit in the comfortable haze of Andy's car, her fingers laced through his. There, for the first time in many weeks, the cocoon of their love felt warm and comfortable, rather than something that ignited fear.

Back at the house, they found Ellen and Will both seated on the floor with a box of pizza in front of them. The television screamed a funny comic book-themed TV show Will loved, and the train tracks had formed enough lines to span a continent. Ellen grabbed another slice, hugged Beth goodbye, and paraded back into the night. Beth's heart ballooned with love for her boys, there in the house where she'd built the only life she had known for years. Maybe this life had nothing against Axel's multi-million-dollar one, but it was hers.

With Will's focus on the television, Beth showed Andy the letter from the lawyer along with the phone number she was meant to call to arrange the paternity test. Andy insisted on calling the man who'd dropped off the documents.

"You don't have to do this all alone," he told her as he lifted his phone.

Beth listened with bated breath as Andy greeted the man coldly. It was decided that he would bring some of Will's hair to the man in an envelope, where he currently stayed at a nearby hotel. The paternity test normally released results within a week. Beth knew this week would stretch out like a million of them lined up together.

After the phone call, Andy suggested wine, which Beth refused. "I want to stay clear-headed," she explained. "I don't want to spiral."

After Will's show ended, Andy started a movie, which allowed the three of them to curl up on the couch. Andy popped popcorn in the microwave and portioned it out in little blue bowls. Will was captivated by the movie and hardly touched his snack. His captivation soon gave way to exhaustion, however, as his head fell against the nearest pillow and he was cast into sleep.

Once Will slept, Beth snipped some strands of his hair and slipped them into an envelope. She hated doing it to his perfect bell haircut and tried to make sure the locks were taken inconspicuously. Afterward, Andy lifted him into his arms and carried him to bed, where he slipped him beneath the covers with the ease of a father doing it for the five hundredth time.

"Let Andy in," Ellen had told her. "Let us help you."

Maybe this Axel situation had forced Beth's hand. She needed help more than ever. And here Andy was, with strong arms and enough love to carry them through.

Beth and Andy collapsed back on the couch. Neither of them remembered what had happened in the movie they'd started, but neither suggested rewinding to figure out what they'd missed. Beth took a small kernel of popcorn and chewed thoughtfully.

"I just don't know how I'm going to get through the next week," she whispered.

Andy took her hand and laced his fingers through hers. "Life's about distraction, isn't it? We'll find little ways. We'll build an even bigger line of train tracks across your living room. We'll bake plenty of cookies and eat them till we're overstuffed. We'll tell my family the wedding's off for now and watch them freak out..."

"Ha." Beth had to admit that this last one sounded particularly funny. "I hate killing their dreams like this."

"Come on. You're not built like my sisters," Andy told her. "Charlotte and Claire are obsessive when it comes to this stuff, and I love them for it. But I love you for you, too."

Beth grumbled inwardly. "The thing is, I used to be like them. As a kid and a teenager and an early twenty-something, I dreamed about my wedding all the time. I wanted it to be perfect. But then..."

"Life had its way with you," Andy finished her sentence.

"I couldn't get excited about flower arrangements or china plates or string quartets after that," Beth offered. "That's not to say your family hasn't had their share of hardships."

"We all deal with it differently," Andy said as he wrapped his arm over her shoulder and cuddled her close. "We all have our crosses to bear."

Beth burrowed her head against Andy's chest and listened to the thump-thump of his heart. Deep within her belly, Andy's child brewed up more and more cells, carving out space in a world that was sometimes terribly dark and sometimes terribly beautiful. One day soon, they would share the wonder of having a child. Hopefully, the chaos in which they now lived would calm soon, and she would find a way to live in total honesty.

CHAPTER SEVENTEEN

FOR THE FIRST time in ages, Andy awoke at Beth's home as the grey light of the morning cascaded through the slats in the window blinds. Beth remained asleep: her lips parted slightly as she dove through the final scenes of whatever dream she'd had. The alarm would ring out in thirty minutes, announcing the brutality of a brand-new day. Just now, Andy was allowed the beauty of the in-between.

Since he and Beth had agreed to push back the wedding to an undetermined date, both he and Beth had breathed a collective sigh of relief. Their love continued to bloom between them, finding new heights and new depths. In many ways, it reminded Andy of a tree growing in a forest, its roots creeping through the soil to latch onto the earth and its limbs reaching toward the skies above. Before she awoke, Andy pressed a kiss onto Beth's forehead. He wanted to press pause before the rest of their life began. He wanted just this.

The flurry of the morning at Beth's house was rather exciting

and ornate posts on all four corners. He imagined them spending their lives in that bed— nursing one another back to health, making love, and maybe, one day, even creating a new baby.

Andy as a father. He'd hardly envisioned this. He'd imagined himself only as a lonely veteran and nothing more.

The front door of the warehouse slammed closed and snapped Andy out of his reverie. He returned to his work on the bookshelf and glanced up briefly as Clint stomped past. He slammed a bottle of whiskey onto his work table, fetched a glass, then added maybe a shot and a half. It was only one in the afternoon and already, Clint had committed himself to the in-between of drunkenness.

"You okay?" Andy finally mustered.

Clint grunted in return. He drank the rest of his whiskey then poured himself another. Andy wiped his hands of wood shavings and followed the older man's gaze up toward the boat, which hung, awaiting its infinite number of repairs.

"I thought that I'd like to make Beth a bed for a wedding present," Andy tried then as a way to fill the space. "Do you think I could use the space here for that kind of project?"

Clint shrugged. "There's enough space."

Andy's stomach grew cold. He returned to his work on the bookshelf, sensing that Clint wanted nothing more than to be left alone just then. For the first weeks of their friendship, Clint had seemed very keen on building a thicker-than-blood relationship with Andy, which Andy had welcomed whole-heartedly. Trevor Montgomery was difficult, especially after their decades of disputes. Clint had seemed to see through Andy's veteran soul.

An hour or so later, Andy lifted his eyes back to find that Clint had collapsed onto a stool, a glass of whiskey still in hand. It was difficult to gauge how many whiskeys this now was for him. His eyes remained peering into space. On closer inspection, Andy realized the older man was crying.

Andy placed his tools back on the table and stepped lightly toward Clint. There, he took a glass for himself, filled it with whiskey, and sat alongside him, staring into the same space as though he could see what Clint saw. Andy knew better than most that sometimes, all you needed was someone to sit next to you in silence when you felt your worst.

After what seemed like twenty minutes, Clint finally spoke.

"I haven't heard from Axel since the other day. I've reached out to him about the potential of going over the blueprints again. I need to finalize the next steps of this stupid boat, but I don't want to do anything without his agreement. It's meant to be his. It's meant to be my gift of love to him. When he approached me about making it, I was overjoyed. Finally, I thought, he needs me. He wants to mend whatever it is we had."

Andy's eyes grew heavy with sorrow. "You know he's trying to get confirmation that Will's his son?"

"He's a stubborn guy. Short-sighted sometimes and pretty obsessive," Clint said then with a subtle shrug. "He's probably created a whole story in his head around Will. And there's really no changing his mind once it's started."

"Beth's freaked out. I don't know what to tell her."

"I wouldn't know what to say, either. Except she slept with the wrong man," Clint said.

Andy was stumped after that. There wasn't anything to say.

"If he really wants this young man to be his son," Clint began now, "I wish he would see how ironic it is that I wait here for his call. He's after Will. He's hungry for what it means to be his father. And that's exactly what I tried to do with this stupid boat. I need Axel. I need him to look at me and know me before I leave this damn world behind. I can't explain why I feel that way. Maybe it's just this human thing about wanting to be really known."

Clint tossed back another shot of whiskey and wavered dangerously on his stool. Andy watched him like a hawk. The last thing either of them needed was a terrible tumble.

Andy wanted to tell this man that he wanted to know him.

But he wasn't sure if the words were enough against the weight of feeling this sorrow about his own flesh-and-blood. Instead, he stayed true to his instincts and kept himself quiet.

"They're doing the paternity test?" Clint asked then.

Andy nodded. "Should have the results in a week."

"A week? Science has really come leaps and bounds, hasn't it."

Andy laughed. "Beth and I just said a week feels like a lifetime."

"A week is a lifetime. An hour is a minute. These expressions of time mean very little, don't they? We just keep going. It's all we can do." Clint swiped a hand over his blotchy eyes and then added, "I can't work anymore today, can I? What a sad sack I am."

Andy made the executive decision to close down the warehouse for the afternoon and drive Clint back to his place, where he lived alone in a little cabin with a view of the waterline. The cabin was quaint and tidy and almost assuredly something Clint had built up himself, with all his woodworking abilities. It reminded Andy of a little cottage in a fairytale.

Before Clint got out of Andy's car, he took a staggered breath and said, "Thank you, Kid. It means a lot to know someone's looking out for me in this wicked world."

"Of course," Andy told him, feeling sheepish.

"You know, it occurred to me that if that kid's Axel's..." He trailed off. "If he's really Axel's, then I guess he's my grandson. How about that."

He then kicked open the door and moved his drunken form toward the front door. Andy held his breath as the old man slipped through his unlocked door and disappeared into the shadows behind it.

A real grandfather for Will.

Wasn't that some kind of gift for all of them?

CHAPTER EIGHTEEN

ONE WEEK LATER, Beth received word from Axel's lawyer. Just as she'd known in her heart of hearts, the paternity test was positive. Axel Isaacson was, just as he'd always been, Will's father.

"As you know, Axel Isaacson is interested in building a relationship with his son, given the circumstances of his emotional health," Jack Froth explained over the phone. "We would like to arrange a meeting for later in the week."

Beth's heart hammered against her ribcage, threatening to shatter the bones. Will buzzed past her in the kitchen with an airplane on high. His lips puckered up and made an airplane sound as he went. His mind had escaped to other lands; he seemed far above these strange circumstances. How could a man like Axel ever understand him? How much did one-half of a chromosomal set actually matter?

"I can't make any agreement just now," Beth retorted. "I'm getting Will ready for school."

"You can arrange something later with my secretary," Jack Froth told her. "But know if you don't call back today, we will be in contact tomorrow and the next day and so forth and so on. If you make things difficult, there will be legal consequences."

Susan had said this man was one of the most powerful lawyers on the east coast. Beth could feel the sinister arrogance behind his words. He was accustomed to winning.

Beth hung up the phone and gasped for breath. Will blinked up at her, his blue eyes enormous, as he asked, "Are you all right, Mommy?"

"Just fine, baby. You about ready?"

Once in the car, Beth's vision blurred with tears. She parked the car at the drop-off and helped Will slip his backpack over his shoulders as he described his plans for his art project later that afternoon. She yearned to live forever in that conversation, one of simplistic action and funny color decisions. When she kissed him on the cheek goodbye, she willed herself not to full-on weep.

With Will safely in his classroom, Beth drove the ten minutes to the hospital. Once there, she collapsed in the break room as the other staff members whirled around her in the mania of the early morning. Ellen asked her how she was, which was a question Beth couldn't even begin to answer. Maybe she said, "Fine." Maybe she said something else. Either way, Ellen had to run off for her first appointment, and Beth had to prepare for hers, as well. Emotions just had to wait.

During a two-hour break in the afternoon, Beth found herself guided by an unseen force. She dabbed lipstick over her lips and leaped into her car with a destination in mind: the cut-de-sac at the southern end of Edgartown, where her current nemesis, ex-lover, resided in his multi-million-dollar mansion.

She couldn't have fathomed what the sight did to her when she came upon it. The brick house seemed the direct antithesis of everything she'd built in her and Will's world. Guilt made her fumble with the gear shift. Had she truly given Will the life he deserved? Should she have included Axel every step of the way? Might he have made it so Will hadn't turned out the way he had?

No. She couldn't acknowledge these feelings, even as they lurked beneath the surface of her anxious soul.

Beth made her way up the front steps and pressed the doorbell, armed with a level of bravery she hadn't known she had. After only ten seconds, she buzzed the bell again. Whatever coziness in which Axel now lurked, she wanted to drag him out of it, just as he'd done to her.

Finally, the door opened to reveal the villain of her personal horror story.

Axel was dressed in houseware: expensive-looking sweatpants and a Hanes t-shirt. His ocean-colored eyes were sterling and bright, and his hair was thick and ruffled, as though he hadn't yet showered. He looked at her without shock, as though shock wasn't something he gave out lightly.

"Good afternoon," he greeted. He towered over her in the doorway, a wall between her and the rest of his beautiful home.

"Not so good, actually," Beth returned. "Can I come in?"

"I don't see why that's necessary," he told her. "My lawyer's been in contact with you about arranging a meeting. I think it's best that we handle everything through him."

"And I think handling everything through a lawyer sincerely negates the very particular nature of our situation," she returned, trying on language she'd never used before. She wanted to embody Susan Sheridan.

The very edge of Axel's lips quivered as though he wanted to smile.

"You're different than I remember you, Bethie."

Beth's nostrils flared. Nobody in all her years had called her that save for Axel Isaacson.

"Are you going to let me in? Or should I wait out here on your stoop ringing your doorbell till you call the cops?"

Axel's eyebrows lifted. He stepped back, opened the door wider, and allowed her entrance into his glorious foyer, with its marble flooring and immaculate hanging modern art paintings. Beth had never understood modern art, as she felt it lacked the emotional core of other art. She'd also supposed everyone else saw something she didn't, as though she was too stupid for it.

"Let me make you a cup of tea," Axel said.

"Not necessary," Beth said as he clipped the door shut.

"No niceties, I suppose. But doesn't that negate the very particular nature of our situation?" Axel mocked her.

Beth had no patience for this man. She crossed her arms over her chest, inhaled deeply, and said, "Who do you think you are, coming into my world and destroying the life I've built for Will and me over the past ten years?"

"That's quite bold of you to say," Axel told her.

"Boldness seems to be your game. Going to a lawyer. Demanding a paternity test," Beth blared back.

Axel's laughter was sinister. "There's a real boldness in having someone's baby without ever mentioning it to him."

Beth's cheeks flashed with heat. "What was I supposed to do? You left the island. I never thought you'd come back."

"Maybe I would have, had you called me back," Axel returned. "It wasn't your right to make that decision for yourself. There were two parts of that equation."

"Not in my mind. You made it pretty clear that you wanted nothing to do with the island long-term. You hated your father. Hated that he wanted to build a relationship with you again after everything he'd done to your mother."

"He was and is a stubborn bastard," Axel retorted. "My mother had every right to leave him the way she did."

"Maybe listening to you talk so badly about your father gave me the feeling that you didn't want to be a father yourself," Beth returned.

"I never said that," Axel said, his tone flat. "Admit it, Beth. You want to be seen as this superhero mom who did it all on her own. You don't want to admit that you might have done something wrong in keeping me out. You don't want to admit that maybe, you hurt Will along the way."

"You don't even know him. You don't know me."

They had entered dangerous territory. Axel spread his fingers out and ran them through his dark locks.

"You're selfish, Beth. You were even selfish back then about your torment. So upset about your brother's death— blaming it on yourself all the time, as though it was all about you."

Beth's hand formed a fist. How dare he throw her youthful

emotions back in her face! She'd grown up; she was so different than she'd been at twenty-five. How could he pretend to know?

"Will and I don't want you here. We're doing just fine without you. And his diagnosis? It's much more complicated than you could ever understand."

"Environmental factors," Axel blared back at her. "I've read some literature regarding the subject."

Beth's other hand formed a fist. At this, Axel chuckled.

"Are you going to punch me, Beth? You're five foot one and no more than a hundred and ten pounds."

Beth took in a deep breath, then exhaled as she closed her eyes. She needed to calm herself as she acknowledged the general silliness of this situation. She stood in the mansion of her ex-lover as he dug into her about her decade-old decisions. Toward the back of the house, a sporting event blared announcements from a radio or television. Axel seemed alone in this huge space, with maybe thirty rooms to call his own.

For the first time, Beth considered the fact that Axel might not have anyone in the world to call his own.

This was difficult to face. When Beth had met Axel at the bonfire party ten years before, he'd seem like the pinnacle of success: good-looking with countless friends and a real handle behind the wheel of a sailboat. It had seemed outside the bounds of reason that he even wanted to spend a minute with her, let alone entire nights in her bed.

Throughout all these years, Beth had had Will. It had been just them against the world.

Now, they had Andy. They stood like a powerful force against everything else.

"I'm going to push this for a long time, Beth. It could break you," Axel warned her now.

Beth opened her eyes to form slits. How she hated this man. How strange that that hatred now worked its way toward compassion.

"You can meet him," she finally mustered. "But I need to make sure he's okay with you. He's not always okay with strangers."

"And I think that's a flaw that you've created and allowed him to have," Axel retorted.

Beth lifted a finger to stop him. "You know so little about this or us. Reading 'literature' about autism is very different than living with a child with autism for over nine years. You have to have patience with us if you want to know us. Is that clear?"

Axel's eyes grew shadowed. He rested his hands over his thighs as he assessed her.

"Will's my everything," Beth told him pointedly. "You taking him is like taking a piece of my soul. I need you to respect that. And I need you to know that I will do anything to protect him."

"I hear you, Bethie," Axel said finally.

They exchanged schedules and decided to meet the Saturday before Thanksgiving, which was already five days away. Axel seemed pleased but also skittish, as though he hadn't actually imagined she would let him get away with this.

"What do you think we should do together?" Axel said as Beth prepared to leave. His tone was much different, like a younger man showing his insecurities.

Beth contemplated this, trying to envision her son with this man she'd once thought she could love.

"Will has a lot of magic up his sleeves," she said finally. "He'll guide the way if you let him."

With that, she stepped back into the November afternoon and headed back toward her car. Against all odds, she felt somehow lighter, as though she'd just faced a demon and lived to tell the tale.

CHAPTER NINETEEN

ANDY HADN'T SEEN Clint touch the sailboat in over a week. He'd spent the majority of his time on a particularly heinously difficult armoire, which a client based in Boston had ordered specially from Clint Isaacson, "the best antique dealer on the east coast." Clint grumbled her words as he lifted his sanding machine back to the wood at hand, his eyes still bleary from a recent shot of whiskey. Andy felt he watched a man on the brink of some kind of emotional collapse. All he could do was watch with sharp eyes, praying the tumultuousness would calm soon.

Andy scrubbed his hands clean in the bathroom of the warehouse and then returned to the cathedral of antique furnishings to find none other than Beth Leopold wandering the makeshift halls. Her eyes were hollow and glittering, and when she spotted Andy, she waved to him sheepishly, as though he'd caught her in the midst of something difficult to explain.

"Hey there!" Andy greeted her warmly with a hug. "I didn't expect you."

"I didn't expect me, either. I just thought, well, I didn't know what to do with myself. So I came here."

"How did he seem?"

"Will? Or Axel?"

"Will. Or both, I guess."

Beth's eyes widened. "Will was fascinated with Axel's place. I walked around behind them as Axel showed him all the rooms and his elephant figurines from his trip to India and his massive book collection and here's the kicker— a super-expensive train set, which Will fell head-over-heels for."

"I can imagine," Andy said with a grateful laugh. "Wow."

"Yeah. I hovered in the corner of that train set room for over an hour and watched as Axel and Will swapped very particular details about different kinds of trains. It seems like they're both broadening each other's knowledge."

"Did Axel seem taken aback with Will?"

"I'm not sure he's so experienced with kids to know that Will's that much different," Beth said contemplatively. "Anyway, Will actually asked me why I was still there, like he was already comfortable with Axel. I mean, he's always asked me about his father, and here he was— the man he always dreamed about. I told them I would run an errand and be back in twenty minutes. Twenty minutes feels like it's pushing it, but I left Axel my number and your number and even Ellen's number, just in case."

"It sounds like it couldn't have gone better," Andy pointed out.

"Against all odds..."

"And you trust him?"

"He seems genuinely interested in our son," Beth breathed. "And Will wants nothing more than to love his father. It's a strange thing, allowing this to happen."

"You've covered your bases," Andy said as he rubbed her shoulder lovingly. "And I think you're doing the right thing, taking this outside of court."

"I just don't want Axel to get too big for his britches, thinking he has more right to Will than he does," Beth whispered. "And I don't want Will to fall in love with him only for Axel to leave all over again. Axel's home isn't here. He's a visitor. And I don't know if Will should have to handle that kind of back and forth. That said, Will does have to learn about the nature of people and of life, right? That you can't trust everyone. That..." Beth trailed off and placed her fingers at her temples, rubbing them gently. "Gosh, I must sound like a crazy person."

"You don't. You sound like a worried mother," Andy returned. "Want a glass of water?"

Beth followed Andy like a lost child toward the little kitchenette, where they found Clint sipping back a glass of whiskey. He looked at Beth with hollow eyes. She greeted him and turned her eyes to the floor.

"Will's with Axel today," Andy said to Clint now, not willing to lie.

"Is that right?" Clint didn't sound interested in the slightest. Instead, he yanked himself back toward the larger warehouse room. A moment later, there was the cry of his machine as he swung through another slab of wood.

Beth sipped her glass of water as Andy tried and failed to make conversation. Obviously, her head wasn't in the right place for it.

Finally, she told him to get back to work, as she knew he had a number of projects he wanted to complete before Thanksgiving.

"I'm headed to Mom and Dad's after this," Andy said as he headed back to his machine. "Mom insisted I help with house decorations, and Claire and Charlotte have some dinner planned. Why don't you come by after you pick up Will?"

Beth wiggled her shoulders slightly. "I just don't want to promise anything, just in case things get hairy with Will."

Andy's heart felt slightly bruised. Beth had avoided hang-outs with his family all November long. Probably, she didn't want to face the fact that they'd pushed back the wedding.

"Okay. I understand," he told her. "But you'll call me if you need anything? I don't have to hang decorations all evening long and listen to my sisters swap shopping tips."

Beth laughed good-naturedly as she stood to kiss him. "You can come back to my place after if you want to. I'll fill you in on everything."

"I'd better get up-to-date on all my train knowledge if I'm meant to compete with this other guy in Will's life," Andy teased.

Beth rolled her eyes. "No. Will loves you." She paused, then added, "I heard him praying about you the other night."

Andy was caught off-guard at the words. He'd never imagined that a child would care for him so much that he'd take to God above to ask for his protection. It was so tender.

"Go!" Beth said as Andy continued to ponder this. "I don't want to take up any more of your time with my panicked state. I'll see you later." She then glanced at her phone and said, "I've been gone only twelve minutes, but I think that's about enough for my nerves." She turned on a heel and disappeared through the antique furnishings, her raven-haired ponytail swatting to and fro as she went.

————————

"ANDY! I NEED YOU IN HERE!" His mother stood at the top of a stepladder with her arms outstretched on either side as she tried to align the traditional holiday family Christmas photo at the top of the dining room wall, over the head of the table for all to see as they overindulged over the holiday season.

"Mom, you know better than to do this yourself," Andy teased as he hustled up. Kerry's arms collapsed, and he caught the photo just in time. He beckoned for her to step down the ladder and give him the space required.

In the kitchen, Claire and Charlotte squabbled over what appetizers to make first for the evening ahead. Rachel, Gail, and Abby had a similar squabble over which songs to play on the speaker. Steven walked in to the dining room and said, "A little higher on the right, Bro," as Andy positioned the photograph. And back in the living room came the sound of Kelli in conversation with their father, who answered her questions regarding the real estate business, which Kelli now excelled in alone, without the help of her ex-husband. As though the flurry of activity wasn't enough, Xander arrived that moment with a large box of Frosted Delights donuts, which Claire screeched at, saying, "We have enough food, Xander! Don't you know better than to bring something like that in here?" But before they knew it, everyone had a donut in hand, suggesting that they would make room for whatever other food was thrown their way.

"It's really shaping up in here," Kerry commented from the doorway between the dining room and the living room. With Christmas only four weeks away, she'd already discussed heading out to the Christmas tree farm to select the perfect Montgomery Christmas tree. The previous year's Christmas had been a flurry of panic, as Trevor had been in the hospital. She wanted to do it all right that year.

Andy made his way down from the ladder and breezed into the kitchen, where Claire placed a piece of cheese in his hand and said, "This gouda is divine. You have to try it." Andy placed the cheese on his tongue and closed his eyes against the sinful, fatty, dense salty flavor. "Are we going to be the kind of people who say 'divine' now?" he teased her as Charlotte cackled.

"Hey! Is Beth coming by?" Charlotte asked as Andy scrubbed his hands in the kitchen sink.

"Not today," Andy returned, although this time, his heart didn't maintain any of its initial heaviness. He and Beth seemed on the same page regarding everything now. It seemed the first time that Beth had truly allowed him access to her.

"Oh, that's really too bad," his mother cooed from the counter, where she scuttled through a selection of cookie cutters.

"We're really going to make Christmas cookies already?" Claire asked.

"I just thought it would be nice for some of the kids..." Kerry countered.

"Mom. All of our kids are teenagers or older," Charlotte countered.

"Which means they eat everything in sight," Kerry returned firmly. "I told you. I want this Christmas to have everything last

Christmas didn't. I promised myself in your father's hospital room that if we managed to make it to this year..."

"If we what?" Trevor paraded into the kitchen after that. He slipped into the fridge, grabbed a domestic beer, and twisted off the top before he placed a kiss on Kerry's cheek. Although the old man could be difficult, with enough mean streaks sizzling through him to last a lifetime, his love for his wife was everlasting. It had provided the base for their children and their children's children— and would be felt in all dimensions of their future generations.

"Oh, you. You're just about as useless as they come," Kerry told him brightly. "What do you think about Christmas cookies?"

"I think I'd like to eat about twelve of them right now," Trevor told her.

"You two are impossible," Claire said with a heavy sigh.

Hours later, the Montgomery family sat around the dinner table for Claire and Charlotte's specialty: enchiladas. They sizzled and spat in their glass pan as Claire delivered them to the table.

"My goodness, these look delicious," Kerry breathed.

"Mexican food?" Trevor demanded, who was accustomed to being a meat-and-potatoes kind of guy.

"Come on, Dad, you'll love them," Charlotte offered.

Andy had fallen into a kind of trance over the previous few hours. His ears had curled around his sisters' little fights, finding them humorous rather than annoying. He'd craved his mother's laughter, which rang out through the house every few minutes. He'd cracked a few beers with his father and his older brother, Steve, as they talked about a recent sporting event on the wrap-around porch, looking out across the ocean.

Someday soon, Andy knew, Beth would be amongst them.

Someday soon, his family would join together with this family. His mother would bake up little cookies for Will, making sure to stir up his favorite flavors and overstuffing him till Beth had to fight her off. This was the grandmother way.

"It really is too bad about Beth not making it tonight," Kerry lamented mid-way through dinner as she toyed with the melted cheese that gooped from her enchilada. "I really want to include her in every bit of this holiday season. Especially since you said, you wanted the wedding sometime after Thanksgiving... Gosh, there's so much to do! Charlotte and I discussed making our own cake..."

Andy stiffened. The air over the table shifted slightly as all eyes turned toward him. He placed his fork on his plate, swiped his napkin across his mustache (because if he had sauce on his mustache during this confession, he would never live it down), and said, "Actually, Beth and Will are having a pretty tumultuous time right now. I don't want to go into it. But it's looking like we'll push the wedding back indefinitely."

Kerry's jaw dropped open. Silence remained like a heavy cloud over the table. Andy met his mother's gaze and tried to fix it up the best he could.

"But really. You'll all know the minute it happens."

"Oh, honey. I'm so sorry..." Kerry breathed as she pressed her hand over her cheek.

"Is there anything we can do for Beth? Are you still together?" his father demanded.

"We're still together. We're doing everything together," Andy recited.

"Won't you tell us what's going on so that we can at least try to help?" Charlotte asked. "It makes me feel like my hands are tied when you're going through so much together..."

"I knew something was up that day we went dress shopping," Claire admitted. "She just looked so lost."

"She's not lost," Andy blared suddenly. "We're just trying to take everything one day at a time. There's no rush. We love each other..."

Andy's eyes flickered toward Kelli, who'd remained silent throughout this strange diatribe.

"You don't have so long to decide, though, right?" Kelli said then as her eyes widened.

Kerry's jaw dropped still lower. "What on earth is that supposed to mean?"

"Long?" Andy repeated. "I don't understand."

Kelli dropped her eyes to her half-eaten enchiladas and took a long sip of wine.

"Kelli? Are you going to explain what you mean by that?" Kerry demanded, using her formal, mother-knows-best tone.

"Yeah, Kelli. Are you going to explain?" Andy crossed his arms over his chest and glared at her. Kelli's cheeks flashed pink with embarrassment.

Now, the silence across the Montgomery family seemed deafening. Kelli kept her eyes toward her food as though praying that time itself could march backward to an era when she hadn't opened her big, stupid mouth.

Something clicked within Andy's mind after that. He felt many puzzle pieces swimming together and forming what, perhaps, a part of his gut had known for a little while. He hadn't seen Beth drink a single glass of wine, something she loved to do, in ages.

CHAPTER TWENTY

AXEL'S CLEANING lady let Beth back into the house approximately sixteen minutes after she'd left it, feeling half-foolish at her over-reaction. The cleaning lady did a sort of up-down with her eyes, assessing Beth's torn jeans and V-neck t-shirt as though she wasn't entirely sure why her boss, the illustrious and mesmerizing Axel Isaacson, would be caught dead around the likes of this rag-tag thirty-five-year-old. Probably, Axel's kind of women these days was in her mid-twenties with set-aside time to shave her legs and pluck her eyebrows.

"They're still in the train room," the cleaning lady said. "The boy can be very loud."

Beth's stomach curdled as her smile fell from her face. "Thanks."

"Shoes off," the cleaning lady instructed as Beth sauntered across the foyer, but Beth ignored her and headed back toward the belly of the great mansion to find her son. As though she'd planned it, her shoes accidentally squeaked against the marble. She thanked God above.

Will and Axel's conversation had maintained its nerd level. Beth paused outside the doorway to listen to Will's familiar charade of dinosaur information as Axel asked appropriate questions, his voice lilting. There certainly was tenderness to this man— something Beth couldn't have sensed from her initial interactions over the previous weeks. That said, he had been incredibly kind to her during that summer: kissing her forehead, making her coffee before she rolled out of bed in the morning, listening as she cried about her brother...

He'd turned dark and sour in the interim. Perhaps it wasn't permanent. Or maybe, as he so frequently did, Will had enacted a bit of his magic upon his father, drawing out the good and canceling out the bad.

When Will took a deep breath between dinosaur tales, Beth knocked her knuckles against the doorway and peered in. Axel and Will had positioned themselves on two separate bean bags and faced one another with a half-finished, mostly-forgotten board game between them on the floor.

"Mom!" Will jumped up and rushed to her, throwing her arms around her with excitement. It had been only seventeen minutes, but Beth was grateful Will had found space to miss her, even as he'd dug into his budding relationship with his father.

Axel took a moment to clamber out of the beanbag. Once up, he placed his hand at the base of his back and grunted, "I ain't as young as I used to be. Not sure why I thought I could sit on a beanbag like that."

Will belly-laughed as Beth assessed the energy between them.

Will was all in one piece. Axel seemed interested and amused and mentioned something about time "flying by." Beth's heart hammered with a mix of relief and, admittedly, a little bit of jealousy. She hadn't expected them to get along like this.

"Why don't you get your stuff together?" Beth asked Will gently after a pause in the conversation.

"We're not finished with the game yet," Will countered.

Axel shrugged. "Just a half-hour more, maybe?"

Beth grimaced as Will gestured toward an easy chair in the corner. "Axel has so many books. Maybe you could read until we're finished?"

"You a reader, Beth?" Axel asked.

"When I have the time," Beth admitted. She hadn't had the time in many months, it seemed like. She turned toward his bookshelf and perused his many titles: crime thrillers and scary stories and old biographies of long-dead soldiers. Meanwhile, Will and Axel fell back into their game, teasing one another with "trash talk" as they went.

Beth had the funniest feeling as she sat down with a book. The three of them were a family. There they sat, spending time together on a Saturday, much like so many other families across the United States of America. Why hadn't she wanted something like this? Had she been terribly wrong not to include Axel?

With each glance up from her book, Beth recognized that Axel allowed Will to win the game. When he finally did, Will leaped from his beanbag and performed a little goofy dance, which seemed to delight rather than embarrass Axel. Will hustled to his mother to announce Axel's defeat.

"That's great, honey," she told him. "I'm so proud of you."

to the task of helping her? Or was he also a bit messed up, like she was? Had Kurt's death and Andy's time at war crafted the most unideal parenting team?

No. She couldn't think like that.

If she gave power to these thoughts, they had every potential to come true.

TO BETH'S SURPRISE, Andy's car was parked at the side of the road outside of her house. Her heart jumped into her throat at the sight. Will clapped his hands excitedly and leaped from the vehicle to scamper up to greet Andy, who now opened the front door and waved out. Although his lips spread to accommodate a smile, his eyes didn't reflect the same emotion. Why wasn't Andy still at his parents' house for their cozy family celebration? Why had he already come to hers? She'd expected a listless night in, probably catching up on bad TV when Will went to bed, waiting for Andy to come by when he could.

Andy didn't hug her when she entered. This was another alarming fact. Instead, he allowed Will to drag him into the living room, where he chatted amicably about his "father" and the activities they'd done together. "He's a really cool guy," Will explained, as though it was as factual as the sun rising in the east. "He's going to help me set up a whole new train set next time I see him."

"That's really cool, bud." Andy dropped down on the ground with Will as Will grabbed another board game from the corner. His eyes flashed up toward Beth but immediately lost her gaze.

"Who wants hot cocoa?" Beth said as she snapped the stovetop on.

"Me!" Will called.

Andy didn't bother to respond.

It remained akin to the Cold War in that living room long past Will's bedtime. When Beth finally coaxed him between the sheets, fear caused sweat to bubble up on her upper lip. Was it possible that Andy had come here that evening to break up with her? She'd already pushed back the wedding. Axel was now in the picture, complicating things. Why would Andy want to stick around for such a tumultuous journey?

Andy sat on a stool with a beer in front of him and his arms folded over the countertop. The television was black and shining, reflecting back the opposite image of the living room and kitchen. Beth's heart thudded with apprehension. She wanted him to say whatever he'd come there to say.

Finally, after what seemed like an impossible eternity, Andy cleared his throat and said, "I love you, Beth."

"I love you, too."

"But I... I learned something tonight. Something that made me understand our relationship is a bit like a long-distance one. It's like I'm on this side of the Atlantic Ocean and you're on that other side and we're yelling at each other from shore to shore, trying to communicate without any success."

Beth's eyes shimmered. Andy took another sip of his beer and closed his eyes.

"Beth, I never imagined I would ever be a father," Andy whispered.

God, Kelli had told him.

169

She'd allowed everything to crumble.

Why, then, didn't Beth feel any kind of rage? Perhaps she was too tired for it. Perhaps too much had happened already.

Beth stepped toward the counter and placed a hand over Andy's arm. Andy's eyes were wet and wounded. She still didn't know what to say and kept praying that the appropriate words would land on her tongue.

"I'm really frightened that there's a bigger reason at play here for why you didn't tell me the truth," Andy whispered.

Beth licked her lips. "There's not. Really." She hardly heard her own voice. "I was so overwhelmed with everything going on. Will's tantrums were getting worse. The wedding was approaching. And then suddenly, Axel..."

Andy nodded, but his eyes remained unchanged. Beth's heart shattered.

"I love you, Andy. I love you and I love this baby. I'm just still not sure how it's all supposed to fit together, and I'm freaking out. I'm freaking out! I don't want to make all the same mistakes again. I want to be the perfect mother and the perfect wife—that is, if you still want to marry me someday."

"I want to marry you. I want to help you raise this baby. Why do you think you'll be doing this all on your own? Beth, we're a team. I'm your partner in all things. When will you get that in your head?" Andy whispered.

The words sizzled with intensity. Beth dropped her head as a sob escaped her lips. Andy rushed around the counter and flung his arms around her, allowing her to shake against him.

"I love you, Beth. I love this baby. I'll be there for you and the baby and Will for the rest of my life. I'll be steadfast and loyal and strong in the face of whatever adversity we face."

Beth drew her head back and blinked up into Andy's eyes. Her throat tightened so much she thought she might throat.

Was it possible that she could hope for something better than had ever come before?

Was it possible that her life was about to open up brightly, like curtains drawn on either side of a window to allow for the light to come in? She and Will had had beautiful times, enough love for the two of them to sustain each other for many years. But it was time to make space for something more.

Andy's chin quivered. "You're pregnant with our baby, Beth. I can't believe it."

Beth couldn't hide away her smile any longer. "I can't believe it, either. It's too good to be true."

"I thought we were careful," Andy let out a laugh then a sob.

"I guess not careful enough," Beth told him.

"Thank God," Andy said before he dove forward and showered her with kisses. "Thank God for our recklessness. This is the best gift in the world."

crackers, which he placed before her at the counter as she shifted over the stool.

"I'll be just fine," she said. "But I'm not so sure about that pancake."

Andy flung back to the now-blackened cake as Will walloped with laughter. Andy slid the pancake into the trash cake and took a deep breath.

"That's the thing about life, William," he explained in a fake, formal, father-like voice. "When times get rough, try, try again. Try as many times until you get it right. And then, you'll be rewarded with the perfect pancake."

Beth helped Andy clear out the apartment over the course of the next few days during her lunch break. The warehouse had closed for the week, with Clint saying he needed a "mental break." Andy reached out to Clint a handful of times over these days to check in but received only text messages of approximately three words in length. "I am fine," or "No worries here." Clint had given Andy a great deal of clarity into his emotional state over the previous weeks. Now, it seemed, his words were all dried up. Probably, he'd allowed himself space to dig into one whiskey bottle after the next. Andy prayed for the strength to help him forward after the Thanksgiving holiday— whether that meant asking him to look at his alcohol intake or driving him to AA.

It was easy to find space in Beth's place for Andy's things. She wasn't a fashionista like his sisters and hadn't bothered to use all of her closet prior to his move-in, anyway. He placed his tools in the garage, his guitar in the living room, and his winter coat in the front closet. In a moment, it was like the puzzle piece of "Andy's existence" had clicked fully into Beth and Will's world. He canceled his lease at the shoddy apartment place and fully prepared his mind for the next phase of his life.

Husband. Father. Caretaker. Friend.

THE MORNING OF THANKSGIVING, Beth arranged a newly-ironed shirt across the bedspread. Andy had never had a woman iron him a shirt before. It felt oddly intimate and reminded him of his mother, who'd ironed his father's shirts on Sunday night before the workweek began.

"I could get used to this," Andy admitted.

Beth laughed. "Don't get used to it, but look. I got Will a matching shirt. You two will be picture-perfect."

"This is probably the last year Will will allow anyone to match him," Andy said with a laugh. "At ten, he'll be too grown up."

Beth gave him a fake-pout after that. "Don't remind me he's growing up. Not on Thanksgiving."

Around eleven-thirty, that morning, Will, Andy, and Beth piled into Andy's car and headed off to the Sunrise Cove Inn, where the Montgomery and Sheridan families gathered together for big-time holidays. Will was armed with a number of books and toys, just in case, he wanted to retreat to a side room due to his anxiety. The Sheridan and Montgomery families loved him to pieces— and he echoed back that love. It simply came at too high a pitch, sometimes.

"What is my father doing today?" Will asked from the back seat.

Beth glanced toward Andy and winced. "I'm not really sure."

Will clucked his tongue. Since the previous Saturday, Will had already hung out with his father twice more – once with Beth's complete supervision and the second time completely without. There hadn't been complication. In fact, it was now difficult to remember that Axel had sprung this whole potential legal battle upon them. He seemed soft.

"Why do you ask?" Beth tried asked her son.

"Well, I don't think he has people the way we have people," Will recited.

Sometimes, the boy was so in-tune with the rest of the world, articulating things it seemed unlikely he should have known.

"What makes you say that, honey?" Beth asked.

"Because he said he doesn't have a family," Will told her.

Beth puffed out her cheeks.

"Maybe we could just text him to tell him Happy Thanksgiving?" Will said.

Andy stopped at a red light a few blocks away from the Sunrise Cove. Beth met his gaze as she muttered, "What do you think of this?"

Andy tried to emulate what he thought his mother might do in this instance. In her mind, probably, she would think that it was Thanksgiving. And everyone deserves to feel love on Thanksgiving.

Even still, he understood Beth's hesitance to share her son with this stranger.

"A text can't do any harm," Andy finally said.

"No harm at all!" Will called from the back.

Beth grumbled inwardly and removed her phone from her purse. Will recited the words she wanted him to include in the message, which she showed Andy for approval before the final send-off.

BETH: Will says, 'Happy Thanksgiving.' I wish you a beautiful day of too much food. What are your plans? Love, Will.'

"Looks pretty good," Andy said as Beth winced again before sending.

Only thirty seconds after she sent the message, Beth received a response, which she allowed Andy to read rather than reading it aloud for Will. Andy parked in the parking lot of the Sunrise Cove and read it twice.

AXEL: Hey Will! Happy Thanksgiving to you, too (and to your mom). I don't have much planned for today. What do you say we meet up?

"I don't know," Beth breathed.

"What don't you know?" Will asked.

Andy gripped Beth's hand. "You have to do what's right for you."

"But I don't know if what's right for me is really right," Beth told him. "I don't know if it's selfish."

That moment, Kerry and Trevor Montgomery parked alongside them, both waving wildly through the tinted windows. As Beth and Andy had burrowed themselves away in Beth's place the past few days, they hadn't yet faced his parents in the wake of the big pregnancy discovery.

As a result, the minute Beth appeared alongside the car, Kerry hustled around and threw her arms around her, already full-on weeping.

"Oh, Beth! Beth, I never could have imagined I would become a

brother, Wes, teasing him about a long-ago Thanksgiving celebration at the Sunrise Cove.

"You were maybe six or seven at the time," Kerry said, "And Mom was looking everywhere for the pumpkin pie. She was panicked, the way she sometimes got when everything wasn't just as perfect as she'd pictured. Eventually, we found you seated in the hall closet with the pie on your lap and tons of pumpkin gunk on your nose. You'd taken the mixing spoon and decided to have yourself a little pre-Thanksgiving feast."

Wes guffawed with laughter. "Why can't you remember a story about me that's actually not embarrassing?"

Kerry placed a hand over his patchy head of hair and wiggled it around, teasing him. "That's not what older siblings are for, Wes. We're here to make trouble. Even into our seventies."

As the Sheridan-Montgomery clan stretched across many tables, Charlotte and Claire had done what they did best: assigned seats for everyone to keep things organized. Christine appeared with a bottle of wine and poured glasses for Andy, Kerry, and Trevor, then placed the bottle on the table while she lent congratulations of her own to Beth.

"Our babies will be so similar in age," she said excitedly. "Plus, Baby Max. A whole new generation of kids running around and turning our hair grey."

Beth laughed outright.

"Plus, Will will be the greatest big brother ever," Christine said under her breath.

"We're still waiting to tell him everything," Beth said softly. "It's a difficult time of change for him, and we want to do everything smoothly with perfect communication."

"Perfect communication," Christine repeated. "Never heard the concept before."

Beth and Andy chuckled and glanced at one another in full agreement.

"It's an aspiration," Andy offered then. "Nothing we've managed to reach yet."

"I guess it's a journey like everything else," Christine told them. "Life is long. And I guess we're allowed to make many mistakes before we get it exactly right."

"Let me know when you get it exactly right," Kerry said with a crooked smile as she lifted her glass of wine. "I'm still learning, myself."

CHAPTER TWENTY-TWO

WILL PICKED his way through a slab of turkey, a bit of mashed potatoes, a small portion of green beans, and a butter-smeared roll. Beth picked at her own food sparingly as morning sickness threatened to toss her back to the bathroom, where she'd spent the better portion of the previous week. Axel had texted to suggest that he pick Will up between the main course and dessert and share his own dessert with his son. Beth's heart had felt bruised at the idea. But the third time Will asked about his father's Thanksgiving, Beth lifted her phone to text her agreement to the plan. Axel was alone; Will wanted to see him. Compassion had to force her to grow beyond the walls she'd previously built— somehow.

"Is my father almost here?" Will asked as he clattered his fork back onto his plate.

"He should be here in the next ten minutes," Beth told him.

"Good," Will affirmed as he took another delicate bite of biscuit.

flickering fireplace, announcing that they wanted to play a tune for everyone.

"I don't know about that," Lola called. "I'd like to keep my hearing for another year, thank you very much."

"You stop it," Wes teased.

"You want to do Neil Young?" Trevor muttered to the other two.

"Heart of Gold?" Zach asked.

"Yeah. Sounds great," Trevor affirmed.

"One. A two. A one, two, three..." Zach counted them off, which allowed them to spring forward into this beautiful, nostalgic tune from Neil Young's 1972 album, Harvest.

Beth leaned against Andy as the two of them swayed in time to the music. The Sheridan-Montgomery crew was captivated. Beth's eyes swam across the crowd, taking stock of every member and every friend. Toward the far back of the crowd stood Stan Ellis, who'd recently become friendly with the family, decades after he'd been the man behind the wheel of the boat when Anna Sheridan had died. His affair with Anna had sent shards of glass through the lives of the Sheridan family. Their forgiveness seemed outlandish and powerful. Beth wished she could emulate it in all things.

But strangely, at this moment, all she wanted to do was be with her mother, father, and Kurt again. Perhaps that ache for her first nuclear family would never really go away. Perhaps she was grateful for the power of that love, even though it had left a vacuum in her soul.

Beth's phone began to vibrate mid-way through the Neil Young song. She yanked it from her pocket as fear draped over her shoulders. The only person bound to call just then was Axel.

Beth hopped back to the foyer of the Sunrise Cove, where she answered the phone with a high-pitched "hello."

In the background, Will's cries were like a wild animal's.

"Beth? Beth, I don't know what happened." Axel sounded different than she'd heard him. Unsure of himself. Lost. "We got back to my place and then there was an ambulance at one of the neighbor's. Sirens blaring, All these people outside."

"Oh my God," Beth whispered. She'd witnessed Will have meltdowns for much lesser noises, obviously.

"I don't want to put him in the car," Axel continued. "And I don't want to take him outside to see the chaos at the neighbor's again."

"I'll be right there," Beth told him. "Do your best to talk him down. Tell him that sometimes, people get sick. Sometimes..."

Suddenly, Will's cries got louder. If Beth had to guess, Axel had attempted to place the phone next to Will's ear so that he could hear her. Will didn't take kindly to this, either, as he seemed to whack the phone out of Axel's hand with a clatter.

Andy appeared in the foyer with their coats in hand as though armed with a sixth sense. He flashed the keys from his pocket as Beth hustled to the door and sprung out into the chill, not bothering with her coat. Once in the car, she explained to Andy what she knew thus far.

"Bad luck," Andy breathed. "An ambulance? Gosh. Axel didn't have a chance."

"I know." Beth closed her eyes and tried to calm her anxious breathing. "I hope your mother didn't notice me run out of there like that?"

"Mom's all bleary-eyed over Dad's guitar playing. I'll explain everything later."

Axel lived fifteen minutes from the Sunrise Cove Inn. Andy crept the car down Pleasant Ave, a road that seemed to lead directly into Katama Bay. On the left-hand side was the aftermath of the ambulance's arrival, with ten people gathered outside in conversation, despite the chilly slice of the cold.

"How awful to have such a tragedy on Thanksgiving," Beth whispered.

They parked outside of Axel's mansion as Andy gave the slightest of whistles in acknowledgment of its size. Beth scampered out, dragging her coat along with her as she whipped toward the front door. Andy was right behind her. Axel pulled open the door immediately, as though he'd had an eye out for her the entire time. And a second later, Beth fell in front of her darling Will, who was all curled up on the floor of the dining room, tucked beneath the table. Above him sat a clumsy-looking baked apple pie. Beth wondered if Axel had baked it himself.

"Shhh, baby. It's okay." Beth collected Will in her arms, cradled him, and teetered back and forth.

Axel and Andy appeared in the doorway to the dining room and stood like mighty shadows. Will's eyes closed as he allowed himself to be held and comforted. Soon, the nightmare would end within his mind. Soon, he would find clarity again.

"I was so scared, Mom," he told her finally as he leaned back and swiped a hand over his tear-soaked cheek.

"I know, baby. I would have been scared, too."

Beth asked Axel for a glass of water. He reappeared with water, juice, wine, and scotch, seemingly wanting to cover all bases and not truly knowing how. Beth helped Will sit upright in a dining room chair as Axel beckoned for Andy to join them. Together, the four of them sat like a strange, hodgepodge family. Maybe this was what Thanksgiving was all about.

"You feeling better, buddy?" Axel asked Will tentatively as he poured him some juice.

Will nodded without speaking. He lifted the glass of water and drank half of it without looking up. Axel looked clueless.

"This pie looks delicious," Beth said then.

"Why don't we all have a piece?" Axel said, grateful to have something to cling to.

"That sounds great," Andy said brightly.

Axel disappeared to grab plates, a knife, and four forks. Beth watched his unsteady hand as he cut several uneven pieces.

"I've never baked before. Maybe you can tell," Axel said, picking fun at himself in a way Beth hadn't assumed possible.

"It doesn't matter as long as it has apples and sugar," Beth told him kindly.

Will's appetite had returned. He tore through the first one, then the second slice of pie and thanked Axel warmly. Axel looked as though he'd invented the first wheel.

"Do you mind if I lay down for a little while?" Will asked Beth after he licked his knife clean. "Then, I'd like to go back to the party, if you don't mind."

Beth dismissed him. Together, the three adults watched as Will padded into the living room and curled himself into a ball on the couch. In a moment, soft snores escaped his lips. He was free from the chaos of his mind, if only for a moment.

"I can see that now, too," Axel affirmed.

Silence fell between them. Andy gave a side-glance to Axel, who seemed like the portrait of a defeated man.

"Will doesn't always take to me, either," Andy offered then, wanting to extend some kind of olive branch. "It's almost been a year since we met, but he sometimes looks at me like I'm a stranger. I've had to accept that things aren't always so clear in Will's head. It's nobody's fault. It's just the way it is."

Axel buzzed his lips with sorrow. "When I saw him that day at my father's warehouse, I felt like I'd been run over by a truck."

"I never would have imagined you'd feel that way," Beth breathed. "I didn't keep him from you out of malice. I just assumed, well, like most guys, you wouldn't have wanted to be involved."

The shadows beneath Axel's eyes darkened. "The thing of it is, I don't know if I would have cared. Things were really different for me back then. I had all these aspirations for myself."

"I remember," Beth offered quietly. "You had dreams I couldn't even understand. And it seems like you've made them come true." She gestured around the grand house as proof.

"Things changed for me," Axel continued. "I met a woman who I loved very much. Naomi. We were married six years ago, at the height of my career. Everything was going better than I ever could have imagined. And Naomi wanted a baby. Whatever she wanted, I wanted, too. But we struggled at first. After a few months, we did what any couple might do. We went with IVF. Two rounds. Then another. We had almost given up hope when it finally happened. She was pregnant, and we were over the moon."

Andy's heart thudded with apprehension. This story could only go in one direction.

"Nine months later, we were all set to welcome our baby girl," he continued. "Pink and white room, all decorated by Naomi. We even had a name picked out, Chloe. I had all these images in my head of the world I'd build for her. I would give her everything. Teach her everything. Be the father I felt I'd never had."

Clint's face appeared in the back of Andy's mind. He tried to shove it away, but the truth of it was, Clint was a central theme of this story, even if he hadn't wanted to be.

"But the childbirth was difficult. We were up all night and into the next day. I never imagined in a million years it would go the way it did. Naomi didn't make it. And our baby— our baby was in the NICU for many days before she left this world, as well. Suddenly, I found myself with more money than God himself, yet nobody to love. Nobody to care for."

Andy closed his eyes against the trauma of this story. It was too much. When he opened them again, he watched as Beth closed her hand over Axel's on the table. It wasn't a romantic gesture; if anything, it was a show of compassion. It was just all she could do to ensure he knew she was right there. That he wasn't alone any longer.

"I had no idea Will was out there," Axel continued softly. "And now that I know him, I can't let him go. I hope you understand that."

Beth's eyes glistened with tears. "I don't think he'd let you let him go, Axel. He's wanted a father his entire life. Now, suddenly, he has two. What a lucky kid."

WHEN WILL AWOKE a little bit later, it was decided that they would all return to the Sunrise Cove for more dessert, wine, and conversation. Will grabbed Axel's hand and began to chatter about something they'd discussed previously about trains. Axel jumped into the conversation immediately, with the zeal you'd want from a father.

"I thought we could invite one more person to come," Andy said suddenly, just as they headed for the door.

"Like who?" Beth asked.

He stopped short in the foyer and found Axel's eyes, the same ocean blue as Clint's.

"I really think your father should be there, Axel. He wants to mend things. He's alone in the world and filled with regret. I don't see why you shouldn't give him this one final chance to make things right. He loves you so much."

Axel held his gaze for a long time before he spoke. Andy only assumed he would tell him that Andy didn't know what the hell he was talking about. But after a long pause, Axel nodded, turned his face toward Will's, and said, "Would you like me to invite your grandfather?"

Will's resounding "yes" echoed wall-to-wall throughout the mansion.

It was decided that Beth and Will would head back to the Sunrise Cove Inn to rejoin the festivities while Andy and Axel headed to Clint's cabin to pick him up. Andy was terrified as he slipped into Axel's BMW. There was no telling the state in which they would find Clint, who still hadn't answered Andy's latest text.

"My father was a mountain of a man," Axel muttered as they drove. "I never understood him and Mom filled us with all these stories about him that made him out to be a big villain. If my brother knew I was headed there now to pick him up for Thanksgiving Dinner, he'd ask if I'd had a lobotomy."

When they reached the cabin, Andy stood back behind Axel as Axel knocked on Clint's door. The first knock rang out through the house ominously. The second seemed almost a joke. Axel spun around and brought his arms skyward as he said, "Well, at least we tried."

At that moment, there was a rush of leaves as someone stepped through the overgrown forest just right of the cabin. Clint appeared between the limbs. He looked grizzled and grey yet soberer than he had the week before, with a bright tint to his coloring that ignited Andy with hope. He stopped short when he realized the identity of his visitors.

"Well." He wrapped his hand around his beard and tugged at it. "Well," he said again, as though coming up with something meaningful to say in the midst of so much heartache was about as useless as anything else.

"Dad." Axel took a tentative step forward. "I wanted to invite you to Thanksgiving today with Andy's family."

Clint's face twisted. "Thanksgiving Dinner?"

"Plenty of food," Andy countered. "Turkey and stuffing and mashed potatoes and gravy. We've got enough pie to feed us till Christmas. And my family's a whole lot— like a circus masquerading as a family, but there's a lot of love and warmth there. We'd love it if you came."

Clint's blue eyes returned to Axel's. He grunted inwardly.

"And this is something you want, Axel?" he demanded.

Axel nodded somberly. "I've gotten to know Will a little bit,

family had reached that familiar holiday stage of being painfully annoyed with one another while also feeling unsure of how to go back home and be without each other. Thanksgiving leftovers were reason enough to gather all over again. That and Kerry's insistence that they already watch a Christmas movie together to start out the proper holiday season right.

That morning before their departure to Trevor and Kerry's, Andy and Beth had sat Will down and told him about the pregnancy. Andy's stomach had twisted into knots during the hours beforehand, as he'd feared Beth would land on another panic and demand that Andy return to some shoddy apartment somewhere to give her and Will space. Andy wasn't willing to go down that road again.

Remarkably, Will had taken the news with stride.

"My classmates said this would happen," he explained. "And I did not like it at first. But I got to thinking about all the things I can teach a new baby— about trains and sailboats and cars and other stuff I like. Plus, my friend said this is what people in love do. They make babies."

Beth had blushed at the statement, seemingly lost at the idea that her son might be able to handle a strange shift in the tide.

"Are you going to get married?" Will had asked then, his eyes widening.

Now, at the Montgomery household, Will sat cross-legged on the floor, coloring in a coloring book, while his grandfather watched football on the big screen. Beth chatted amicably with Charlotte, who sat alongside her with a bridal magazine stretched over her legs. Andy had taken a turkey sandwich against his best wishes and now chewed it slowly as he gazed out at his beautiful family— at

Steven and his son toward the back of the room, sipping beers, and Kelli and her daughter doing one another's nails at the little side table, and Kerry bustling in and out to make sure everyone was taken care of. How had he gotten so lucky to have this world?

Andy stepped out onto the wrap-around porch to watch the ocean, which caught the soft light as it hauled its frothy waves toward the beach. November clouds brewed over them, heavy and dark, acting as a reminder that soon, their lives would be nothing but dense snow and darkness.

When Andy turned back to head inside, Beth appeared in the doorway, all bundled up in her adorable winter coat and hat. She slipped her fingers through his and said, "I just wanted to see what it was like outside. And here you are."

"Here I am."

They held one another's gaze as the door slammed shut behind them. Andy's heart felt so heavy with the immensity of his love for her.

"I can't believe how well that went this morning," he said.

"Me neither. And that thing about getting married? Here I've been, trying to tend to Will's feelings in everything, only for him to show me how much he can handle." Beth shook her head to allow her raven curls to toss over her shoulders.

"Your mother showed me something upstairs," Beth said suddenly, lowering her voice.

"You sound secretive. Is Mom making a bomb?"

Beth cackled brightly as she tossed her head back. "Don't ever stop making me laugh, Andy. Okay?"

"It will be my honor to make you laugh for the rest of my life," Andy told her firmly.

Beth allowed the silence to fall again. Finally, she said, "Your mom found your grandmother Marilyn's wedding dress. The one she wore when she married Robert. She made me try it on..."

Andy's jaw dropped.

"Anyway, it's basically a perfect fit," Beth murmured shyly. "And I was wondering... well. Basically, everyone that we wanted here for the wedding is here. And now that Will's given us the okay, and you've moved all your stuff in, and I'm only going to get bigger from here on out..."

Andy's eyesight grew blurry with tears understanding what she was trying to say. He took her hands tenderly in his. "If you want to marry me today, how could I refuse?"

THE FLURRY of activity of the next two hours was unmatched in the history of any holiday-making cheer in the Montgomery household.

Everyone got to work. Kerry cleaned the kitchen; Steven set up chairs on the porch; Charlotte dragged Beth upstairs for makeup and hair duties; Claire raced off to the flower shop to arrange something last-minute; and Gail, Abby, and Rachel set about cultivating the perfect wedding playlist, as per usual.

"Something tasteful and classy, girls!" Charlotte cried before she disappeared upstairs.

Andy felt at a loss and unsure of where to put his hands. Never in his life had he thought he would actually find the woman he wanted to settle down with. Now, here she was. He would marry her within the hour. Sometimes, life jumped up to grab you— and all you could do was go along for the ride.

Kelli changed into a dress, placed her glasses on the bridge of her nose, and brought up the vows on her phone. Trevor then insisted she print them out, which resulted in a whole bunch of half-curses from the family computer as Trevor tried to remember how to make the printer work. Finally, Kelli reappeared with the print-out, her face a mix of exasperation and good humor.

"I hope Beth knows what she's getting into," she teased.

Andy's suit remained in the old family house, something he'd had to purchase the previous Christmas after his return home. He slipped it on easily and assessed himself in the mirror. Steven marched up behind him, still in a baseball hat, and wolf-whistled.

"My baby brother. All grown up."

"Yeah, it's hard to believe at thirty-six I finally have to grow up," Andy said sarcastically.

The portion of the back porch with walls and closed-in windows was center-stage for the ceremony. It was decided that Will would walk his mother down the aisle. He took this assignment with great courage and stoicism. He was grateful, beyond that, that he was forced only to wear a button-down shirt rather than a suit, which he said was usually "too itchy."

By the time Claire reappeared with enough champagne to fill several bathtubs and a bouquet for the bride-to-be, everyone had gathered out on the enclosed porch in preparation for the spontaneous wedding of the century. Charlotte burst into the porch area with panicked yet excited eyes.

"I thought my Thanksgiving wedding last year was rushed," she

Made in the USA
Las Vegas, NV
27 April 2022

48069930R00115